Awareness sizzled in the air

"I don't normally do this." Sara seemed to hesitate. "Okay, I never do this. But would you like to come upstairs?"

Michael's body hardened, his mind leaping ahead to the two of them naked, entwined in her bed. He dropped her hand and stuffed both of his into his pockets. "This isn't smart, Sara. We just met. You don't know anything about me."

She laid a hand against his cheek, her eyes asking him to trust her. "Why don't you tell me?"

Here was his chance to do the right thing. She thought he was a hero. A hero! It was almost laughable.

He opened his mouth, closed it, then opened it again. But all he managed to say was "I'm not the man you think I am...."

Dear Reader,

How much stock do we put in the opinions of others? That question led me to write *The Hero's Sin*, about a man viewed as anything but a hero.

I got the idea to have a town newcomer, who has no preconceived notion of our antihero, witness him bravely churning through white water to save a boy from drowning. Once unflattering portrayals of him reach her, she has to decide what to believe. Her ears? Her eyes? Or her heart?

The Hero's Sin is the first of three books set in the fictional Pennsylvania mountain town of Indigo Springs. But the beauty of the countryside, with the dramatic peaks and the tumbling river, is very real.

I hope you enjoy the visit to Indigo Springs as much as I enjoyed creating the town—and the heroine's dilemma.

All my best,

Darlene Gardner

P.S. Visit me on the Web at www.darlenegardner.com.

THE HERO'S SIN
Darlene Gardner

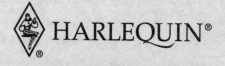

HARLEQUIN®

TORONTO • NEW YORK • LONDON
AMSTERDAM • PARIS • SYDNEY • HAMBURG
STOCKHOLM • ATHENS • TOKYO • MILAN • MADRID
PRAGUE • WARSAW • BUDAPEST • AUCKLAND

Recycling programs
for this product may
not exist in your area.

ISBN-13: 978-0-373-78289-5
ISBN-10:   0-373-78289-6

THE HERO'S SIN

www.eHarlequin.com

Printed in U.S.A.

ABOUT THE AUTHOR

While working as a newspaper sportswriter, Darlene Gardner realized she'd rather make up quotes than rely on an athlete to say something interesting. So she quit her job and concentrated on a fiction career, which landed her at Harlequin/Silhouette Books, where she's written for the Temptation, Duets and Intimate Moments lines before finding a home at Harlequin Superromance. Please visit Darlene on the Web at www.darlenegardner.com.

Books by Darlene Gardner

HARLEQUIN SUPERROMANCE
1316–MILLION TO ONE
1360–A TIME TO FORGIVE
1396–A TIME TO COME HOME
1431–THE OTHER WOMAN'S SON
1490–ANYTHING FOR HER CHILDREN

To Lisa Dyson, Beth Fedorko and Diane Perkins,
because they're wonderful

CHAPTER ONE

MURDERER.

The word resounded in Michael Donahue's head. It had been years since anyone had hurled the accusation at him but he leveled it at himself every day.

He bent down and picked up a flat rock, throwing it sidearm so it skipped across the shimmering surface of the Lehigh River before disappearing from sight.

That's what he felt like doing. Disappearing.

He'd come to the river straight from the Philadelphia hotel where he'd been staying since returning from West Africa, so nobody in Indigo Springs had seen him yet. He could get back inside his rental car and put in motion his vague plan to find a quiet place where he could unwind until he heard whether he'd been approved for his next assignment. It didn't matter where he went, as long as it was far from here.

Except he couldn't leave until Sunday morning and it was only Friday afternoon. He had a rehearsal dinner and a wedding to get through because he'd given his word to his boyhood friend Johnny Pollock that he'd show. At least Michael had had the foresight not to let Johnny talk him into being best man.

"Best man," Michael muttered, picking up another rock and chucking it as far as he could.

How ironic was that?

He sat down on one of the large slate rocks that lined the bank of the river, took off his shoes and socks and dangled his feet in the cool water.

He used to come to the river when he was a kid, although Aunt Felicia had probably thought he was off raising hell. She'd had reason. Despite her good intentions, his great-aunt hadn't been able to handle a teenage boy angry at his mother for dying. Neither could she shield him from the loud arguments with her husband, who didn't want him in their house.

Michael sighed, his gaze moving to the opposite riverbank where he spotted a great blue heron. Its spindly legs supported a gawky body more gray than blue. The bird flapped its wings and ascended into the cloudless sky, transforming into a creature of breathtaking beauty in an instant.

He soon figured out the reason the heron had taken flight: a kayak appeared, followed by a string of bright-green rubber rafts heading for the white water slightly downriver from where he sat.

He read the writing on the sides of the rafts as they drew closer—Indigo River Rafters, one of the outfits that operated guided commercial white-water trips on the Lehigh. The companies catered mostly to tourists, also offering mountain bikes and tubes for rent.

Chrissy had been partial to tubing.

He tried to blot out the memory, but it took hold. His mind conjured up an image of Chrissy, her blond hair pulled back from her pretty, laughing face as they headed downriver on the inflatable rubber tubes. Not that either of them had paid a rental fee for their fun.

Getting a couple of truck-tire inner tubes from Jessup's Automotive Store in town would have been easy enough, but that's not the way Michael had rolled. He'd wait until the commercial guides were loading tubes back onto the truck, then lift a couple when their backs were turned.

Chrissy had been up for it, but then she'd been up for just about anything. That was one of the things he'd enjoyed about her. He'd liked the way she'd been on his side, too. Maybe that's why he hadn't tried too hard to talk her out of leaving Indigo Springs with him.

He rubbed the back of his neck, wishing in vain that the breeze off the river could blow away his guilt.

The boats were closer now, the rafters following the guide in the lead kayak down the left side of the river where the rapids were easier to ride.

The current was swifter than usual for summer, when the commercial companies were usually relegated to running pleasure trips. He was familiar enough with the river's nuances that he figured it was a dam-release day. Officials periodically released water from the reservoir to increase the flow and depth of the river. The deeper, faster-moving water made for better fishing, boating and rafting, leading to more tourist dollars.

The strategy was working, judging by the number of people on this trip. Michael watched the rafters in front of the pack take their wild ride down the rapid, glimpsing wide grins and smiling, carefree faces.

As he tried to muster the courage to return to the town where he'd never been welcome, he envied them.

MAYBE HER FAMILY was right and she wasn't as adventurous as she claimed to be.

The closer her group of rafters came to the churning, frothing rapid, the more Sara Brenneman felt compelled to paddle against the current. Back the way they'd come.

She suspected the beads of moisture on her forehead were drops of cold sweat instead of water from the Lehigh.

She glimpsed a lone, dark-haired man sitting on a rock, watching the rafts go by as though he didn't have a worry in the world. How she wished she could join him on dry land.

She should be back in Indigo Springs unpacking the boxes that still filled the three-story stone row house she'd recently purchased in the heart of the downtown. The building was zoned commercial, and she was transforming the ground floor into a law office she hoped to open officially a week from Monday.

Only ten days from now.

Everything had happened so fast. One minute she was an associate at the large corporate firm in Washington, D.C., where her father was a partner. The next she was "seriously disappointing" him by starting a new life in a picturesque Pocono Mountains town where she knew no one except an old friend from high-school and the Realtor who had mentioned the white-water-rafting trip.

Even the three people in the raft with her were strangers, although they'd introduced themselves after a pretty guide with a port-wine stain on one cheek had told Sara to form a foursome with an existing group.

The same guide had launched into a talk on what to expect, mentioning that the rapids they'd be riding were classified as Class II and III. That wasn't particularly daunting in a ranking system that topped out at Class V, but the approaching rapid was reportedly the most challenging.

"Just follow the path the lead kayak takes, and it'll be a breeze," the guide had said.

Sara, buoyed by the same spirit of daring that had enabled her to leave her old life behind, had believed her.

Until this moment and this rapid.

If things didn't go well, Sara might be tempted to believe her family knew her better than she knew herself.

The rush of blood pounding in her ears merged with the roar of the white water as she paddled along with the others in her raft through the rapids. Rocks jutted out from the river, their edges appearing as jagged as serrated knives.

The rubber raft ran the gauntlet, bouncing on the water as though navigating the bumps and turns of a roller coaster. Sara's stomach pitched and rolled with every swerve of the raft, and she consciously had to remind herself to inhale. They shot through the final stretch, a film of spray sprinkling the air as exhilaration hit Sara like a splash in the face.

She turned to see how the rafters trailing them were faring, the sun temporarily blinding her before her vision cleared. The raft directly behind them had veered to the right, where the rocks were more numerous, the path more treacherous.

Worse, one of the five people in the raft—a tow-headed boy no older than ten or eleven— perched not on the edge of the raft but smack in the middle, the exact spot he'd been warned not to sit.

The ejector seat, the guide had called it during the safety segment of her pre-trip talk.

Sara spotted the massive rock at the same time as the rafters in the boy's raft. A man and woman Sara presumed were the boy's parents, plus two older kids, paddled furiously to avoid it, but their raft smashed into the unyielding surface of the rock with resounding force.

Horror gripped her heart as the boy went flying into the swirling water of the river. His companions kept paddling, trying to navigate the rapid, seemingly oblivious to what had happened.

"Man overboard!" Sara yelled, but the thunderous howl of the white water drowned out the sound to everyone except those in her raft.

The boy's blond head and the orange of his lifejacket became visible above the white froth. His arms flailed wildly.

Sara frantically tried to remember what the guide had instructed them to do should a rafter fall overboard.

"Feet first!" she shouted, but the boy didn't have a prayer of hearing over the angry rumble of the water. She couldn't even hear herself. "Lie back!"

The boy remained upright, increasing the likelihood his foot would get wedged by a rock. If he got stuck, the water would rush over his head, overwhelming him. And nobody in her raft could reach him, not when they were downriver from the spot where he'd fallen in and the current was running against them.

"Somebody help him!" Panic welled in her throat but she kept yelling. "Oh, please God! Somebody help him!"

A commercial trip like this one should have no shortage of people who could come to the rescue, but the guide in the lead kayak had already moved on to the next stretch of river and a big gap existed between the boy and the rafts bringing up the rear. Even if the guide in the trailing kayak noticed the boy was in trouble, he'd arrive too late.

The boy bounced off a rock, and Sara prayed his vest had cushioned the blow, that his head hadn't taken a hit.

The water swept him along a perilous few feet, but he managed to remain upright. Then abruptly his forward progress stopped, and Sara suspected the worst had happened. He was stuck.

"Help him!" Sara yelled, the sound swallowed by the white water that had turned from beautiful to deadly in an instant.

Panic squeezed Sara's heart. The other people in her raft were also shouting now. The four of them paddled desperately against the current even though reaching the boy was hopeless.

And then she saw a second dark head in the water, moving toward the first. A man this time, but not the man who'd been in the raft with the boy. It could only be the man who'd been sitting on the side of the river.

The man shot through the hissing rapids feet-first, with no inflated rubber raft to protect his body from the merciless rocks, a Lone Ranger tactic that could get him killed. The froth rose up intermittently to obscure him from view, but he moved inexorably closer to his goal.

The boy was fifteen feet away.

Ten.

Five.

And then the water splashed violently against the rocks, spraying into the air so Sara lost sight of both man and boy. She pictured the current sucking them under the surface, their mouths gasping for oxygen, their lungs filling with water. Dread welled up inside Sara like bile, and she shut her eyes against the devastating disappointment.

But when she opened them again, man and boy were moving down the river as one. The man must have hooked his arm around the boy, dislodging him from whatever had pinned him in place. He was guiding the boy away from the rocks, away from the swirling froth, away from danger.

The relentless surge of the white water deposited the boy and his rescuer into the relative calm of the cool, clear pool below the rapids, not far from Sara's foursome and the raft of people who'd only just discovered the boy missing.

The boy was gasping and his young face looked as white as the froth on the rapids, but he appeared to be unhurt. Thanks to the man.

Sara caught a glimpse of a thin stream of blood trickling down the side of a hard, handsome face before the man helped hoist the boy back onto the raft into the waiting arms of the couple Sara believed were his parents.

The current was already taking the rafts downriver from the scene of the rescue. The man swam at an angle to shore, his strokes sure and strong. Sara watched until he reached land and stepped onto the bank, his clothes hanging wetly on his tall, muscular body. He, too, appeared to be okay.

Who was he? she wondered as her raft drifted farther and farther away. But she already knew.

He was a hero.

HE WAS a coward.

Otherwise he'd hang up the hotel phone, change into something besides the faded jeans and T-shirt he wore and drive to the Indigo Springs restaurant where Johnny and his fiancée were holding their rehearsal dinner.

"Yeah?" It was Johnny's voice, barely audible above the buzz of conversation and clinking of silverware.

"Johnny, it's Michael."

"Mikey Mike," Johnny exclaimed, the ridiculous nickname making Michael smile. Only

Johnny could get away with calling him that. "Where are you? We're almost through with appetizers."

Michael swallowed. "I'm not coming."

"What? Hold on a minute." The background noise gradually lessened, and Michael pictured Johnny walking away from the table to find a quieter spot. "What aren't you coming to? The rehearsal dinner or the wedding?"

"The dinner."

"So you're in town?" Johnny asked, his relief evident.

"I will be," Michael said, deliberately vague. There was no point in telling Johnny that, in another cowardly move, he'd checked into a cookie-cutter hotel near the interstate that was a full twenty miles from Indigo Springs. Especially since he'd led Johnny to believe he'd be staying with his great-aunt.

"Want to tell me why you're not coming to dinner?"

Michael didn't, but Johnny deserved an answer. Without Johnny's friendship, life in Indigo Springs would have been even less bearable. Even after Chrissy's death, Johnny had stuck by him, making the two-hour drive to visit him in Johnstown every few months. They hadn't seen each other since Michael had gone to the West African country of Niger two years ago, but the bond they'd formed as teenagers never weakened. Johnny was more like a brother than a friend.

"I've got a nasty bump on my head." Michael gingerly touched the spot where his forehead had come in contact with the edge of a rock. The hot shower he'd taken had washed away the river water and the blood but not the bruise. "I wouldn't be good company, especially in a crowd."

"What happened?" Johnny asked sharply. "Were you in an accident?"

"A minor one." Guilt gnawed at Michael. His head ached, but not enough to keep him from anything he really wanted to do. "It'll be fine by morning."

"You sure?"

"I'm sure," Michael said, then cleared the emotion from his throat. It had been a long time since anyone had been concerned about him. "You'd better get back to your guests."

"And you better show tomorrow, buddy. I let you weasel out of being my best man, but I want you at my wedding, damn it. I'm only getting married once."

"I'll be there," Michael promised.

After disconnecting the call, Michael ignored the nearly overwhelming temptation to turn on the television and switch on the Phillies. He'd gotten accustomed to the lack of electricity in the adobe hut where he'd lived in Niger, but enjoyed few things more than a beer and a baseball game.

Not giving himself time for second guessing, he rode the elevator to the hotel lobby, walked past the bored-looking clerk and headed for the black PT Cruiser he'd parked in the hotel lot. It was the last car he would have chosen but the only one the busy rental agency at the airport had available.

Thirty minutes later, he pulled the PT Cruiser to the crowded curb across from his great aunt's house and set the brake to keep the car from rolling down the hill. Somebody on the street had company, but he doubted it was his quiet, reserved aunt.

His aunt's charming Victorian house was much as Michael remembered it, with flowers hanging from baskets on her wraparound porch and planted in beds in the front yard. But as he trudged up the sidewalk, he noticed that the lawn needed mowing and the porch could use a coat of paint. Aunt Felicia's husband—Michael never had been able to think of the man as his uncle—would normally have taken care of those chores, but he'd been dead for three months.

If Murray were still alive, Michael wouldn't be here.

And then only a screen door separated Michael from the house where he hadn't been able to find refuge. The doorbell didn't sound when he pressed the button so he rapped on the frame and waited. He heard voices and laughter. It seemed he'd misjudged Aunt Felicia, but it was too late to turn back.

"Just a minute." He recognized the gentle, slightly melodic voice of his great-aunt.

He held his ground, wiping his damp palms on the legs of jeans too warm for the balmy summer night. He smelled molasses and brown sugar and guessed she'd baked a shoo-fly cake, her specialty, for her guests. Time seemed to stretch before she came into view. Considerably grayer and smaller than he remembered, she moved slowly toward the door, then stopped as though she'd slammed into a barrier.

"Michael?" Her voice trembled. "Is that you?"

"It's me, Aunt Felicia."

Her hand fluttered to her forehead to the exact spot where he knew his injury was, and he guessed he was black-and-blue. "Your head…"

"It's nothing." He shrugged to underscore his words.

He waited for her to invite him inside, but she just stood there staring at him. His throat felt so thick he wasn't sure he could speak. He hadn't seen her since his eighteenth birthday, the day Murray had kicked him out. That had been nine years ago.

He squinted. The years had taken their toll. Through the screen of the door, she looked every one of her seventy-plus years.

"I thought you were in Africa," his aunt finally said, her voice no steadier than before.

He swallowed. "I only just got back to the States. I thought you should know I'm in town for Johnny's wedding."

He owed Aunt Felicia that much. She'd taken him in during that dark time after his mother had overdosed. Even though his aunt hadn't been able to stand up to her husband in the end, he still remembered her trying to explain.

"If it was just me, you could stay," she'd told him, tears trickling down her papery cheeks. "But I'm worn out from arguing with him about you."

Michael had claimed to understand but hadn't. Not back then. Back then he'd wanted somebody to want him. That's probably why he hadn't protested too long or too hard when Chrissy insisted she was leaving Indigo Springs with him.

Nine years, he thought again. Chrissy had been dead for eight of them.

His aunt didn't say anything now, her mouth working but no words emerging.

He cleared his throat. "Johnny told me about Murray. I'm sorry." It was the truth. Michael didn't wish anybody dead. Not even Murray.

"Felicia. It's your turn." A woman's voice floated from the direction of the living room.

"Bridge night," his aunt explained.

"Who's at the door anyway?" A different, louder voice. One that sounded familiar.

"No one," his aunt replied quickly, the answer stabbing through him like a jagged spear. She blinked a few times, shifted from foot to foot, her hand fluttering to her throat. Her eyes seemed to plead with him. "You understand I can't invite you in."

"I understand." He gave the same answer he had years ago, but this time it was the truth. Aunt Felicia's friends would be Indigo Springs long-timers. She had good reason to be ashamed of him. "I just wanted to be the one to tell you I was in town."

Once he showed up at the wedding, the buzzing would start. It wouldn't take long for word to reach Aunt Felicia.

"Where are you staying?" she asked.

"A hotel outside of town."

"Felicia!" A different voice this time. "We're waiting."

His aunt's face twisted with an emotion he couldn't identify.

"You'd better go," he told her and backed away from the door, chiding himself for expecting too much. He descended the creaky porch stairs and was almost to the sidewalk when her voice stopped him, so soft he almost didn't hear it.

"Michael."

He turned around, trying not to hope. "Yeah?"

"When are you leaving town?"

"Sunday morning," he said.

"Could you stop by before you go?"

He started nodding before she finished the question, a flame of optimism leaping inside him. "Yeah. Sure."

"I've got some of your things in the basement," she said softly. "Nothing valuable, but you might want them back."

Somehow he managed to tell her good-night before making his lonely way back to his rental car. He wished like hell he hadn't promised Johnny he'd come to the wedding.

Some people really couldn't go home again.

It seemed he was one of them.

CHAPTER TWO

"I NEVER saw anybody cry so much at a wedding!"

Sara tried not to wince as she regarded the short, middle-aged woman in front of her in the receiving line at the VFW hall, which was decorated in soft pastels to reflect the varying colors of the bridesmaid's dresses.

So much for creating a first impression of toughness, a quality most people sought in a lawyer.

Sara couldn't even console herself with the fiction that few of the wedding guests had noticed her tears. Three women had offered her tissues. This woman—she'd introduced herself as Marie Dombrowski—hadn't been sitting anywhere near her.

"Weddings do that to me," Sara said as they passed through an arch of silk flowers interspersed with white netting and approached the receiving line. "I can't seem to help myself."

Marie patted Sara on the arm, sympathy practically oozing from her. "Don't worry, dear. Someday it'll be your turn."

"You've got it wrong. That's not why—" Sara began.

"Being a romantic is nothing to be ashamed of," Marie interrupted. "But of course you know that. Only a romantic would wear an adorable dress like that."

Sara smoothed a hand down the skirt of the paisley-print, triple-flounced sleeveless dress she wore with matching pink-and-red-satin sandals. She'd bought the dress on a whim while shopping for a new work wardrobe that wasn't so stuffy. The look was ultra-feminine, a drastic change of pace from the structured suits she used to wear no matter the occasion.

"Thank you," Sara said, "but nobody's ever called me a romantic before. Especially not the men I've dated."

"Then none of them must've been right for you," Marie declared. She herself was wearing a pink knee-length dress with tiny appliquéd hearts on the bodice.

"I wasn't right for them, either. Lawyers don't generally make good girlfriends."

"Now I know who you are!" Marie exclaimed, looking delighted with herself. "You bought that empty storefront on Main Street. Aren't you an old friend of the bride's from high school?"

"That's right. But how did you know that?"

"Oh, honey. Indigo Springs may be turning into a tourist town, but among the locals nothing's a mystery. Isn't that right, Frank?" She nudged the stout, silent man at her elbow she'd introduced as her husband. He startled as though he'd been awakened from a nap even though they were among the last guests to arrive and the decibel level in the hall grew louder by the second.

"Oh, yes." His smile included both Sara and his wife. "Whatever you say, dear."

"In this case," Sara said, "I'm hoping the story about me crying at the wedding doesn't get around."

"Are you kidding?" Marie exclaimed. "That's the only thing people would be talking about if it wasn't for Michael Donahue."

Marie and her husband reached the front of the receiving line before Sara could ask who Michael Donahue was. This wasn't the first time she'd heard the name. While she'd waited outside the church for the newly married couple to emerge, two elderly men had been discussing him.

"You're sure it was Donahue?" one of the men had asked in a loud voice.

"'Course I am. Came in late and sat in the last pew. Slipped out before the ceremony ended, too."

The loud man had whistled. "Wonder what Quincy Coleman will do when he finds out he's back."

Who was Michael Donahue? And who, for that matter, was Quincy Coleman?

Sara put her curiosity on hold as she approached the parents of the bride, who were first in the receiving line and whom Sara had met once before. But the question was still tapping at the back of her mind as she reintroduced herself to Penelope's mother and father and greeted the groom's parents.

Penelope could surely enlighten her about Michael Donahue, but it became apparent now wasn't the time to question her when the bride squealed.

"I'm so glad you're here!" Penelope threw her arms around Sara, crinkling the bodice of her white gown against Sara's chest and enveloping her in the scent of perfume. Penelope drew back and asked, "Is it true you cried through the ceremony?"

Sara laughed. "True. But it was your fault for looking so happy."

"I *am* happy." With her light-brown hair in an updo and eye makeup playing up her huge dark eyes, Penelope looked lovely. She beamed at her new husband, formally attired in a gray pin-striped tuxedo. "I'm the luckiest woman in the world."

"And don't you forget it." Johnny Pollock winked at his bride. He was neither tall nor short, his features neither ugly nor handsome, his hair color neither blond nor brown. He was average in every way—until he smiled, transforming him into something special. "Nice to see you again, Sara."

Sara had barely returned Johnny's greeting when Penelope captured both of Sara's hands in hers. "I never thought you'd leave that big law firm, but I'm so glad you did. I hope you love it here as much as I do."

Love was the reason Penelope had relocated to Indigo Springs. Weeks after she'd made a sales call to Johnny's construction company peddling industrial piping, he'd asked her to marry him. She'd dumped the job and gained a husband.

"I'm already starting to," Sara said.

"Now go circulate." Penelope beckoned her close and whispered in her ear. "I'm trying to figure out who the eligible men are, but forget about Johnny's best man. Chase is hot, but his girlfriend and her little boy are living with him and they have a baby on the way."

Sara rolled her eyes. Weddings, like no other events, seemed to bring out the matchmakers. "I'm starting a career, not looking for a man."

Penelope grinned. "Then I'll look for you. Only not today. I'm a little busy."

Sara moved down the receiving line, but before she got to the best man, who was indeed handsome, a redhead in a tight green dress pulled him aside. The redhead complained loudly that he wasn't paying her enough attention.

The poor guy was trying so hard to get her to lower her voice that Sara pretended not to notice and stepped into the reception hall.

She was used to elegant weddings with sit-down dinners and soft music, perhaps from a classically trained pianist or a string ensemble. A quartet of middle-aged men, including a saxophonist and an accordionist, were setting up what Sara guessed was a polka band near a spacious dance floor. Waitstaff arranged steaming platters of food on a bountiful buffet table.

The VFW hall was loud and crowded, with wedding guests filling up long, skinny tables. Artificial flower arrangements added color to the tables, which were covered in white cloth like the chairs. As a finishing touch, oversized pastel bows had been tied to the backs of each seat. Sara skirted the periphery of the room, searching for a place to sit.

"Over here, Sara!" Marie Dombrowski beckoned her to a nearby spot, where she sat with her silent husband. "Come join me and Frank."

Sara smiled, grateful for the invitation. Before she took a step, something made her look in the direction of the receiving line, which had started to break up as the wedding party made its way to the bridal table. Only Penelope, Johnny and his father remained.

Johnny grinned hugely before embracing a tall man with short dark hair who seemed vaguely familiar. Johnny held on to the other man for long seconds, patting him repeatedly and enthusiastically on the back.

"Are you coming, Sara?" Marie Dombrowski called.

"In a minute." Sara held up a finger, her attention still riveted by the groom and the stranger.

The two men drew apart. Sara had judged Johnny to be five ten or eleven when she'd stood next to him. The stranger topped him by a good three or four inches. His posture was proud, almost defiant, and he wore a gray suit a few shades lighter than Johnny's tuxedo that looked good on his athletic frame.

Johnny's father came forward, embracing the stranger just as enthusiastically as his son had before somebody called him away. Then Johnny grabbed Penelope's hand and pulled her close, no doubt to introduce her. The angle of the stranger's head changed, and Sara got a good look at his hard, handsome face.

She inhaled sharply. If she hadn't been sure of the man's identity, the bruise on his forehead would have been a dead giveaway.

It was the hero from the river.

"YOU'RE AS pretty as Johnny said you were." Michael extended a hand to Johnny's bride, a slender brunette with her hair piled high on her head, wisps of it falling charmingly about her face.

"Thank you." Her eyes flew to his forehead, and she winced. "I see why you didn't come to the rehearsal dinner. What happened?"

"Nothing worth repeating," Michael said. Until she mentioned it, he'd almost forgotten he'd used the injury as an excuse. "Just glad I could be here to see my old buddy get married."

"That's right. You grew up with Johnny. He told me all about you." Her smile seemed genuine, which meant Johnny hadn't told her *everything* about him. "Will you be in town long?"

"I'm just here for the wedding."

"That's too bad. I don't understand why anybody would ever want to leave Indigo Springs. I absolutely adore it here."

Michael felt the muscles holding up his smile tighten. That confirmed it. Johnny hadn't filled Penelope in on the whole story. "I hope you'll be happy here."

"I'll make sure of that," Johnny hugged her to his side.

"Okay, lovebirds, you're needed at the main table." A woman in a flowing floral-print dress called as she bustled toward them. She stopped short, gaping at Michael as though his suit jacket was stained with blood. He mentally subtracted the woman's extra pounds and the gray in her hair and recognized Johnny's aunt Ida. Before Michael could greet her, she looked past him to Johnny and Penelope. "Everybody's waiting on you so the best man can give the toast and people can eat."

She turned away without acknowledging Michael, not that he expected her to, not when he remembered her as one of Chrissy's mother's closest friends. Ida had pledged her allegiance years ago, and it hadn't been to him.

A warm hand clasped his shoulder. "Don't worry about Aunt Ida," Johnny reassured him. "I'm glad you're here. Maybe we can catch up later."

Michael nodded, although there was little chance of that happening at a reception of more than a hundred people. Johnny knew it, too. He slapped Michael on the shoulder. "Good seeing you, man."

"Always," Michael said.

Dropping his hand, Johnny escorted his bride into the main part of the hall to a bridal table decorated with tall candles, fresh flowers and draped garlands.

Michael surveyed the wedding guests chatting happily to one another and knew what it felt like to be alone in a crowd. Most were strangers, but he recognized some of them, none of whom he felt comfortable approaching.

He waited a few beats, then headed for the exit and the parking lot, pretending he wasn't in a hurry. He'd considered himself lucky to find a parking space, but a now a white van blocked his escape route. The scripted red letters on the side of the vehicle read *Catering Solutions: We cook so you don't have to.* The driver's seat was empty.

"Damn." There was no getting around it. He needed to re-enter the hall and locate the caterers, no matter how much it might send tongues wagging.

Even as he lectured himself on the cold reality of his situation, he wished things were different. Wished, for instance, that the woman with the red highlights in her long brown hair was headed for him instead of the parking lot.

He'd noticed her at the church, partly because she wore a ridiculously feminine dress with high-heeled sandals that added inches to her tall frame and showed off a killer set of legs. With a slightly long nose and a wide mouth, she wasn't classically beautiful as much as she was damn attractive. But it wasn't only her looks that captured his attention. It was the poise with which she moved, the intelligence in her expression that told him he'd enjoy getting to know her.

Not that there was a chance in hell of that happening.

Then she smiled.

He checked behind him, but the parking lot and front sidewalk were deserted except for him. It wasn't yet dusk so he'd clearly seen her welcoming expression.

He expected her to keep on walking, for her smile to vanish. But it widened, reaching large eyes the same light brown as the cream soda Aunt Felicia used to buy when he was a teenager.

When she stopped before him, there could be no mistaking it—the smile was for him.

"You're my hero," she said.

He felt the corners of his mouth drop. Was she someone from his past playing a sick joke? She was about his age. About the age Chrissy would have been had she lived. But, no. He didn't know her. This was a woman he wouldn't have forgotten.

"Excuse me?" he asked.

Admiration gleamed in her eyes, as easy to read as the red block letters on the white sign in front of the VFW hall. The members of the Veterans of Foreign Wars were heroes, not him.

"I saw you," she said. "At the river. When you saved that boy."

She *didn't* know him. Didn't know about the sin in his past. The tension slowly left him as he put together the pieces. She must have been along on the raft trip when the boy had fallen overboard into the white water.

"You were wonderful," she added.

He frowned. "I didn't do anything anyone else wouldn't have done."

"Are you joking?" Her cream-soda eyes widened, disbelief touching her lips. "You rode that rapid without a raft. You could have drowned along with that boy."

He shifted from one foot to the other, uncomfortable with her exaggeration. He knew enough about the Lehigh to go feet-first down a rapid, which had substantially lessened the danger. "Yeah, well, both of us made it through okay."

She reached up and traced her fingers lightly against his temple, the gesture kindling a warmth inside him even though her touch was as soft as the brush of a feather. "Except for this nasty bump."

"It's nothing," he mumbled.

Her fingers fell away from his temple, and he squashed a crazy desire to capture her hand and press it against his heart.

"The boy's parents were asking about you. They wanted to know your name so they could thank you." Her smile grew. "I'd like to know it, too, but I should introduce myself first." She stuck out a slim hand. Like her other, it was ringless. "Sara Brenneman. I'm new in town. Haven't been here a week yet."

He folded her hand in his and again felt the warmth. The confidence he'd glimpsed in her walk was also evident in her grip. "Michael Donahue."

He might not have picked up on the way her body tensed if he hadn't been shaking her hand. Modulating the pitch of his voice to disguise his disappointment, he let go of her hand. "I take it you've heard of me."

She didn't avoid the question, which heightened his opinion of her. "I overheard some people talking about how you were back in town."

She didn't recoil, so that was probably all she'd heard. For now. She'd get the rest of the story soon enough.

The silence between them stretched a few beats, then she said, "I hope you're back for good."

That would be unthinkable.

"I'm leaving first thing tomorrow." He didn't tell her where he was going, but then his plan was hazy. He figured he'd head north on Highway 80 until he felt like stopping, possibly somewhere he could rent a place on a lake with access to a boat. The paperwork for his next assignment should come through any day, telling him which exotic nation he was headed to next.

He swore disappointment descended over her features before she brightened. "Then let's make the most of tonight. Will you sit with me at dinner?"

He hesitated, surprised he wanted to say yes.

She grimaced. "Please tell me I didn't make a faux pas and proposition a married man."

Proposition? She'd used the word in a nonsexual context but his body stirred. "Not married, but I'm leaving as soon as I get the caterer to move the van. My car's blocked in."

"The caterer will be too busy to do anything until after dinner," she said. "Besides, you have to eat, right?"

He'd intended to grab a burger at the fast-food restaurant near his hotel. That plan seemed even less appealing with Sara Brenneman waiting for his answer.

"If you say no," Sara said, "I'll have to spend the reception hiding out in the restroom because every matchmaker in the hall is eyeing me."

He chuckled. "You're making that up."

"Am not. Even the bride has me in her sights."

"In that case," he said, going with his gut, "how can I refuse?"

"Good." Her smile reached her eyes, which struck him as sexy as hell. "I want to know all about you."

He braced himself for questions as they walked back inside the building, but she provided answers, telling him about the solo general practice law firm she was set to open and ticking off her specialties: real estate, fore-closures, wills, probates, small business matters.

The best man, a friend of Johnny's who'd moved to town after Michael left, was just finishing the toast when they entered the crowded hall. Panic flashed through Michael as he felt the eyes of the curious bore into them.

Sara had claimed a desire to get to know him better. More than a few people in the reception hall could tell her she wouldn't like what she learned.

THE HERO was uncomfortable.

Sara sensed it in the taut set of Michael's shoulders while she led him to the table where the Dombrowskis waited. Marie waved, flashing the same sweet grin as when she'd invited Sara to sit with them.

Michael's step faltered. "I thought you were here alone."

"I came alone but they invited me to sit with them." She smiled at him. It seemed she couldn't stop smiling at him. And why not? He was as modest as he was heroic. He smelled good, too. Like fresh air and warm skin. "You'll like Marie and Frank. They're new in town, like me. Retirees who like to kayak. And read. Marie wants to get me involved with Friends of the Library."

His steps were still slow, causing her to stop dead. She knew nothing about him except he'd lived in Indigo Springs sometime in the past. She'd gotten the vague impression some residents didn't welcome his return, but other guests had nodded at him in acknowledgement when they reentered the hall.

"I'll understand if you'd rather sit with somebody else." She grimaced. "Be disappointed, yes. But I will understand."

He touched her bare arm, sending pleasure shooting through her. "There's no one I'd rather sit with than you."

Their eyes met, and she felt a connection that was tangible. Marie Dombrowski must have picked up on it, too, because she patted Michael on the hand after Sara performed the introductions. Once done making a fuss over the bruise on his forehead, she said, "Shame on Sara for not telling us she had a date. But where were you when she was boo-hoo-ing through the wedding?"

"I didn't boo-hoo, I sniffled," Sara protested. At this rate, she'd be known as the weeping lawyer before she opened her practice. "Weddings do that to me. And Michael isn't my date. We just met outside."

Marie's mouth and eyes rounded comically. "You mean you left the hall and found a man?"

"Don't knock it, Marie," Frank Dombrowski interjected. "Some women know what they want when they see it."

Sara laughed, even though Frank's observation wasn't far off the mark. "Michael's not a complete stranger. I saw him res—"

"Our paths crossed yesterday." Michael shifted in his chair, his broad shoulders rolling under his suit jacket. He had a naturally soft voice that made everything he said carry more importance. "Sara was nice enough to invite me to join her for dinner."

"So you came alone, too?" Marie addressed Michael. "Don't you live here in town?"

"Not anymore. I'm an old friend of the groom's. How about you, Mrs. Dombrowski? Bride or groom?"

Sara got the distinct impression Michael didn't want to talk about himself, but Marie seemed not to notice. "Groom. Frank and I contracted with Pollock Construction to redo our bathrooms, and we hit it off with Johnny. We just love him."

Marie chattered happily on, taking a break only to fill her plate with kielbasa, pierogis and other Polish foods from the buffet table. The subject of home improvement was obviously a favorite topic. By dinner's end, Sara knew a lot about the Dombrowskis but no more about Michael Donahue than she had when it began.

Sara was trying to figure out how to get Michael alone when the polka band struck its first chords.

Marie jumped up and extended a hand to her husband, who got obligingly to his feet. "I hope you two don't mind if we desert you. Frank and I love to dance."

"Have fun," Sara said, then waited until the couple was gone to remark to Michael. "You don't say much about yourself, do you?"

"When somebody likes to talk as much as Marie," he said, "there's no point in denying her the pleasure."

She suspected there was more to it than that, but she played along. "I told you all about my law practice, but I don't even know what you do for a living."

"I'm in construction."

She was about to ask him to elaborate when the groom's father approached him from behind and clapped him on the shoulders. Smiling, Michael turned.

"I'm glad you're still here." Mr. Pollock was an older, stockier version of his son with an open, engaging manner that was extremely likeable. His twinkling gaze drifted to Sara. "Do I have you to thank for that, Sara?"

Impressed he'd remembered her name after

the brief meeting in the reception line, she joked, "You know what they say about lawyers and our powers of persuasion."

Twin dimples appeared on Mr. Pollock's face, making him look boyish. "Then maybe you can persuade him to stick around for a while. Our boy here's a world traveler. Did he tell you he just got back from Africa?"

Africa?

"I didn't think so," Mr. Pollock said before Sara recovered from the surprise. To Michael, he said, "Please tell me you're staying in the States for a while."

"Can't do that," Michael said. "I already applied for another assignment, probably in Ghana, but maybe in El Salvador."

As they spoke, Sara was aware of other guests watching them. Watching *Michael*. But even though the reception was at least an hour old, only Mr. Pollock had approached him. She wondered why.

"If you ever decide to stay put, you know you have a job with me." Mr. Pollock was about to say more when a willowy girl in her early teens with a mouthful of braces grabbed his hand.

"You said you'd dance with me, Uncle Nick," she said, pulling him away as she spoke.

"Can you believe how shy this girl is," he

called to them over his shoulder, but he was laughing. "Catch you both later."

Michael turned back around in his seat.

"Ghana? El Salvador?" Sara listed the countries. "I thought you said you were in construction."

"*Overseas* construction," he said. "I go where the work is."

"Isn't all that moving around tough on you?"

"It suits me," he said.

"Not me. My dad was a navy JAG so we never stayed in one place for long when I was growing up. I think that's why Indigo Springs appeals to me. You can put down roots here."

He was silent.

"How long ago did you leave?" she asked.

"Nine years." He gave her a wry smile. "And it's time I left again. That catering truck should be gone by now."

"You can't go yet!" Sara reached across the table and placed her hand over his, feeling electricity shoot right to her core. The orchestra began to play a lively tune. "Not until you teach me to polka."

He arched one of his dark eyebrows. "What makes you think I can polka?"

"You and Johnny are friends, so you must have picked it up somewhere along the way."

Her hand still covered his, even though there was no reason for it. She withdrew it reluctantly and stood up, knocking over a half-filled glass of white wine that splashed over her dress. "Oh, no! I need to run to the restroom and blot up this mess. Don't go anywhere, okay?"

She grabbed his arm and looked into his eyes, which were blue-gray, like the color of the river water. He nodded, but didn't reply. She reluctantly let go and hurried to the restroom, casting a glance over her shoulder.

Despite the connection she felt when she touched him, she wasn't sure Michael would be waiting when she returned.

MICHAEL WATCHED the couples on the floor, deliberately not meeting anyone's eyes. As soon as he danced one polka with Sara, he was out of here. He wouldn't have stayed this long if not for that catering truck.

He expelled a short breath. Who was he kidding? The driver had probably moved that truck an hour ago. The reason Michael hadn't left yet was wearing a pink and red dress.

"What the hell are you doing here, Donahue?" The words were slurred, but Michael recognized the voice before he saw the speaker.

Kenny Grieb, the ex-high-school jock Chrissy had dated before Michael. He wasn't as lean or as muscular as he'd been in high school, but the bitterness in his expression was the same.

"I was invited," Michael said.

"You shouldn't have come," Kenny drawled, moving closer as he talked. His floppy brown hair was untidy, his shirt coming loose from his dress slacks, his face flushed.

Michael had never been afraid of Kenny and wasn't now, but put his hand up like a stop sign. "I don't want any trouble."

"Too late." Kenny took another step and nearly tripped over an empty chair. It upended and clattered to the floor, drawing attention.

If Michael didn't get out of here soon, Kenny would create a scene and cast an ugly pall over Johnny's wedding day.

Michael glanced in the direction Sara had gone but didn't see her. Regret seized him that he wouldn't get a chance to say goodbye, but it couldn't be helped.

"I was just leaving," he said.

"That's right," Kenny yelled, his voice competing with the polka music. "Get out and don't come back."

Michael's hands fisted at his sides, but for Johnny's sake he said nothing. He stopped only long enough to intercept Marie Dombrowski and ask her to give Sara his apologies.

Then he left, a prospect that no longer held the same appeal now that he'd met Sara.

Dusk had settled over the town, but the temperature had dipped into what felt like the sixties, downright cool compared to Niger's heart. He removed his suit jacket and loosened his tie, trying not to look back.

That was a problem of his. He usually couldn't help looking back.

The catering truck was no longer double-parked behind his rental car, clearing a path for him to drive away from the reception. Away from Indigo Springs. Away from Sara, who had been a pipe dream anyway.

He took the keys out of his pocket and hit the remote. The lights of his PT Cruiser blinked on, sounding a short, shrill beep at the same time somebody called, "Not so fast, asshole."

Great.

Kenny Grieb had followed him.

CHAPTER THREE

SARA RUSHED BACK to the table, her dress damp from where she'd blotted up the wine. Her round trip had taken longer than expected because Johnny's father waylaid her when she was exiting the restroom.

"Great to see you and Michael hitting it off," Nick Pollock had said. "I get the feeling he doesn't socialize much in the Peace Corps."

"The Peace Corps!" Sara repeated. Why hadn't she put that together herself when she learned of the far-flung places Michael had worked? "He never told me he was a volunteer."

"Didn't think he would. He's sort of a serial volunteer. Been signing up for two-year assignments since he put himself through college. Holding down a full-time job at the time. He probably didn't tell you that, either."

"No," Sara said. "But why are *you* telling me?"

"Because Michael's a good man," he'd said

enigmatically, his expression suddenly serious. "Don't let anyone tell you differently."

"Why would anyone say differently?"

He'd sighed and rubbed a hand over his jaw. "Michael had it tough growing up. Did a couple of things he shouldn't have. Angered some people. But he got through it and turned himself into somebody to be proud of."

Stop talking in circles! she wanted to yell. Instead she thanked him for enlightening her, a sixth sense urging her to hurry back to Michael. His empty chair confirmed her intuition that he'd been about to bolt.

She surveyed the smiling couples twirling around the dance floor as the polka music played, hoping she was wrong, hoping Michael was among them. Somehow she knew she wouldn't find him.

Marie Dombrowski spotted her and separated herself from her husband, her brows pinched together in what looked like sympathy. "Michael asked me to tell you he had to go."

Sara must not have kept the dismay from her face, because Marie squeezed her hand. "I don't think he wanted to leave, but another man—I didn't recognize him but I do know he was drunk—was creating a scene. It seemed to me Michael left so there wouldn't be trouble."

Sara thought over what Nick Pollock had told her, but she didn't have enough information about Michael's past to figure out why somebody would accost him.

"He's only been gone a few minutes," Marie added. "If you hurry, you might be able to catch him."

"Thanks." Sara didn't hesitate, heading for the exit as fast as her high heels would carry her. Before Michael disappeared, maybe forever, she at least wanted to say goodbye.

It wasn't yet fully dark, but the outside lights were on, making it easy to spot Michael in the parking lot. Relief flooding her, she hurried down the sidewalk, then stopped dead. He wasn't alone. A man who had at least thirty pounds on Michael was charging him. The man cocked his arm, drew his shoulder back and let his fist fly.

"No!" Sara yelled, rushing forward to stop the madness.

Michael lifted a forearm, deftly blocking the punch. Then in a lightning quick motion, he grabbed the man's arm and twisted it around his back, effectively incapacitating him.

"Leggo," the man groaned, obviously in discomfort, obviously drunk.

"Not until you understand me." Michael's

low, firm voice carried toward Sara. "If you cause another scene at my friend's wedding, I'll make you regret it."

He released the man's arm and shoved him. The man stumbled backward, nearly falling before catching his balance.

"Go drink some black coffee," Michael ordered harshly.

The man's face, slack from too much alcohol, filled with what looked like hatred. "Go back where you came from," he muttered. "No one wants you here."

It looked as though the man was thinking about initiating another attack, but he rejected the notion, returning to the VFW hall on unsteady feet.

"You." He pointed at Sara as he passed her, his finger shaky. "You should watch who you 'sociate with."

"I didn't ask for your opinion." Without waiting for his response, she walked to where Michael was bending down to pick up his suit jacket from the pavement.

Michael straightened, his suit jacket in hand, and gave her a wry look. "I'm sorry you had to see that."

She looked toward the hall, confirming that the troublemaker had disappeared inside the building. "What I saw was you keeping that jerk from making trouble at your friend's wedding."

"I won't argue with you there. Kenny Grieb's bad news when he's drunk."

"What does he have against you?" Sara asked.

"A grudge," Michael said, "which is why I'm leaving."

She'd half expected him to be gone already when she came looking for him, but his declaration seemed to knock the wind from her. "What if I asked you not to go yet?"

"I wish things were different." His eyes ran over her face like a caress. "But for your sake I should have left hours ago. I'm not exactly Mr. Popular."

She couldn't argue with that, but not everybody inside the hall had been hostile. Excluding the Pollocks, Michael hadn't reached out to a single person. "You're not exactly Mr. Congeniality either."

He stared at her for a moment, then broke into a laugh. "Are you always this blunt?"

"Not always," she said, "but usually."

If she completely spoke her mind, she'd ask for details about why some people had a problem with him. Because she sensed the topic was a raw spot, she could wait until he was ready to tell her.

"Do you have a problem with an outspoken woman?" she asked.

"I have a problem with a woman jeopardizing her reputation in town by hanging out with me."

"What reputation?" she retorted. "I just moved here. I don't have a reputation."

"You should be building one, and a wedding's a good place to start." He gestured toward the hall. "It's not too late. Go network, make some new friends."

"I can make friends tomorrow or the next day or the day after that," she said. "I'm not going anywhere. But you are."

"That's right." He looked toward the parking lot, then at her. If she hadn't read regret in his gaze, she might have let him go.

"You don't have to go until tomorrow morning, right? You don't have anything pressing you need to do tonight? Anywhere you need to be?"

He narrowed his eyes as though it was a trick question. "No," he said slowly.

"Then you can walk me home, because I'm leaving the reception, too." She headed through the parking lot to the sidewalk adjacent to the street, her stomach turning somersaults at the prospect he might refuse. She didn't know why she couldn't let him leave just yet; she just knew that she couldn't. "Coming?" she called over her shoulder.

She reached the sidewalk before conceding that he wasn't following her. She took a deep breath, then turned around. He stood with his jacket in hand, his face half in shadows.

This is it, she thought, a lump forming in her throat.

This is goodbye.

"I can't leave my car here," he said. "Kenny Grieb knows where it's parked."

She released the breath she'd been holding, alleviating the strain on her lungs. Without letting him in on the relief that made her legs feel weak, she strode toward him on her high-heeled shoes.

"Then let's move your car," she said.

MICHAEL FELT as though he'd been transported to an alternate universe.

After Sara directed him to a parking space in a lot adjacent to a real-estate office, they'd taken a sidewalk that led through the heart of Indigo Springs. Despite architecture dating back more than a hundred years, he barely recognized the town.

"Tell me again why we didn't park in the block where you live," Michael said.

"I said you could walk me home, not drive me home," she said. A woman who knew her own mind, he thought.

Restaurants, only a few of which were familiar, were doing a brisk business. Photographers, crafters, glass blowers and painters had taken over previously abandoned storefronts. A bike shop seemed to be on every block. People who looked like tourists strolled the sidewalks.

"What happened to the sleepy town I remember?" Michael asked as they passed the red and white awning of an ice-cream shop. "This hardly seems like the same place."

"It woke up," Sara said. "Mostly because of the mountain-bikers and the hikers. At least, according to my real-estate agent. She said prices are low enough here for people to afford second homes."

Even with the evidence of change all around, Michael had a tough time accepting that the heart of the town was different. Especially when they approached Abe's General Store, a place that seemed frozen in time, right down to the red door with the hand-painted welcome sign.

Memories of his arms being roughly wrenched behind his back and the police taking him away in handcuffs came stampeding back, and he wished he was anywhere but here.

Correction: He wished *they* were anywhere but here.

He couldn't regret spending time with a woman like Sara Brenneman, even though their relationship couldn't go any further than her front door.

"Are you a mountain-biker? Is that why you moved here?" He kept his gaze straight ahead as they passed the general store, unwilling to re-surrect any more bad memories.

"I moved here because I fell in love."

Jealousy hit him hard, a ridiculous reaction, especially because he should have known a woman like her was spoken for. "You have a boyfriend?"

"I meant I fell in love with the town," she said, laughing, and he could breathe again. "At first sight, too. I stopped to visit Penelope on the way back to Washington, D.C., from another friend's wedding. That's all it took."

He waited for a car to pass before they crossed a side street to the quiet of the next block, mostly consisting of businesses that were closed for the day. "Didn't you like living in Washington?"

"It's the fast track I didn't like. I lived in this

great neighborhood near Capitol Hill, but spent most of my time at work. The more hours I billed, the more money the law firm made and the more chance I had of making partner."

"Was that important to you?"

"I used to think so. I told you my dad was a navy JAG, right? Now he's a partner at the firm where I worked. My mom's a pediatrician. I've got a sister in law school and a brother in med school. Everybody's a high achiever."

"So what happened?"

"I woke up one night to a pounding on my door." Her steps had slowed and he matched her more leisurely pace. "I saw a bloody, wild-eyed man through the peephole so I called 911 but didn't open it."

"Smart move."

"Not really. Turned out he lived two doors down and he'd just been mugged. That's when it hit me that I worked so many hours I couldn't even recognize my own neighbor."

"Not necessarily a bad thing."

She shook her head. "For me, it was. I was so busy doing what was expected of me I didn't think about what would make me happy. That's having a social life and feeling like I'm part of a community."

Once upon a time, Michael would have said he

wanted to belong somewhere. But then Murray had booted him out of his great-aunt's house and he'd learned how dangerous it was to want.

"Sounds like you're in the right place." He kept his voice determinedly noncommittal.

"I think so, but nobody else in my family does. They keep saying I'll come back to my senses." She cast him a sidelong glance. "Enough about me. How about you? You keep saying you're leaving tomorrow, but where will you go?"

"To decompress," he said.

A muscle in her jaw twitched, hinting she wasn't satisfied with his short answer. It couldn't be helped. She wouldn't understand that the destination didn't matter as long as it was away from here.

"There it is!" she suddenly exclaimed, clapping her hands like an excited child. "My law office."

She indicated one of the stone row houses that lined the block. It was sandwiched between an insurance office and a dentist, across the street from a small city park that was in shadows.

"I thought I was walking you home."

"I live on the two upper floors. It's the coolest thing. The place is built on a hillside so the office is at street level, but the back of my second floor opens onto a private deck that has a catwalk leading to the woods."

He glanced upward and saw a light shining in a second-floor window.

"Isn't it perfect? Here, I'll show you." She took a key from her little pink evening purse, opened the heavy wood door and flipped on a light.

The setup was typical for a small office. A reception area in front with a pair of offices and a small supply room in the rear. Wood floors and crown molding ran throughout the first floor.

"I need to get it painted and buy some lamps and carpets and artwork. Oh, and get the phone company over here because the phones aren't working. And hire an office manager. I've almost got it covered. I'm going shopping in Allentown tomorrow and I have a couple of job candidates coming in for interviews on Monday."

Her words tripped over each other, and he tried to remember the last time he'd been that excited. He couldn't. She grabbed his hand, leading him to an unusual oak receptionist's desk shaped like a comma.

"Isn't this great?" she asked. "The office furniture came with the place, but I was sure the previous owner would exclude this piece. It's an antique, probably custom-made, too."

"Beautiful," he said, but he was referring to Sara instead of the desk. A light seemed to have switched on inside her as she showed him her office, transforming her from attractive to dazzling.

She turned to him, a sunny smile curving her lips. He tried to mask his attraction, but she must have seen it because the smile changed, its innocence fading. She looked down at their still-linked hands, then up at him. Her hand was silky and warm, the way he imagined the rest of her would feel. The air around them suddenly seemed charged.

"I don't normally do this." She rolled her eyes. "Okay, I never do this, but would you like to come upstairs?"

His body hardened, his mind leaping ahead to the two of them naked, entwined in her bed. He dropped her hand and stuffed both of his in his pockets. "This isn't smart, Sara. We just met. You don't know anything about me."

"I know you risked your life to save a child you'd never seen before. I know you stopped a drunk from ruining your friend's wedding." She raised a hand when he would have protested. "And I know you're in the Peace Corps."

"Who told you that?"

"Mr. Pollock."

Tension gripped Michael's shoulders. "What else did he say?"

"He said you went through a rough patch as

a kid, but you'd rebounded. He said you were a good man."

"He didn't give you any details about my past?"

"Not really." She laid a hand against his cheek, her eyes asking him to trust her. "Why don't you tell me?"

Here was his chance to do the right thing. If he admitted responsibility for Chrissy's death, she'd never look at him with respect and admiration again. She thought he was a hero. A hero! It was almost laughable.

He opened his mouth, closed it, then opened it again. All he managed to say was, "I'm not the man you think I am."

"Then you don't think highly enough of yourself," she said and kissed him.

He had plenty of time to draw back, but he remained in place. Her breath was sweet, her lips soft, her hands at his nape electrifying. His pulse quickened, the passion he'd been keeping carefully in check soaring to the surface.

He should stop this. He'd spent only part of a night in her company, but making love with her wasn't something he'd be able to take lightly.

She snaked her hands around his neck and pulled him closer, molding her body against his. She opened her mouth in a blatant invitation for him to deepen the kiss. He couldn't refuse, his mouth mating with hers as he breathed in her scent.

His hands roamed over her hair, her back, her hips as he kissed her with as little control as the teenage boy he used to be. This was madness. Absolute madness. He hadn't felt so out of control in years, not since he used to wait for Chrissy to sneak out of her house and come to him.

And look how that had turned out.

If Sara knew what had happened to Chrissy, she wouldn't let him kiss her. She'd never again allow him to get close enough to touch her.

With a supreme act of will he broke off the kiss and pulled away from her, listening to the mingled sounds of their harsh breathing. She rested her head against his rapidly beating heart for a moment before stepping out of his arms. He felt immediately bereft.

She took a step toward a stairway that led to her home. To her bed. Her smile was shy. "Are you coming?"

He closed his eyes, trying to shut out the tempting picture she made. But he could still see her, as though her image was imprinted on the insides of his eyelids. He'd probably always be able to conjure up the way she looked right now.

He swallowed, tasting regret, and opened

his eyes. "I already told you, Sara. I want to, but I can't."

Her smile faltered but didn't disappear altogether. "Sure, you can. I already know you're leaving in the morning. You won't be taking advantage of me."

"This isn't you, Sara. Didn't you just say you never have one-night stands?"

"Maybe it won't be just one night. You have friends in town. Maybe you'll come back to visit."

He shook his head. "I won't."

"Then you won't. I'm a big girl. I accept that. I know what I'm doing."

Maybe so, but she didn't know who she'd be doing it with.

Tell her about Chrissy, a voice inside his head urged.

In the end, all he could do was present an argument she couldn't refute.

"I'll probably kick myself for this, but I can't make love to you one day and disappear from your life the next."

She bit her lip, her disappointment as clear as his regret. "I suppose I should thank you for that, but I don't think I can."

"I understand." He stepped forward, laid four fingers against the smooth curve of her cheek. "Goodbye, Sara."

He was halfway out the front door before her voice stopped him. "Michael."

He turned around. She looked almost ethereally beautiful standing in the empty office in front of the antique desk she'd enthused about.

"Mr. Pollock was right," she said. "You are a good man."

He didn't even have the courage to refute that.

THE NEXT MORNING Michael trudged up the narrow flight of stairs that led from Aunt Felicia's basement to the main part of the house, carrying a cardboard box of things he didn't want.

Old clothes that would no longer fit. High-school report cards and test papers that didn't do him proud. A tattered baseball glove he'd found lying discarded in a field when he was a teenager.

He'd already decided to donate the stuff to a thrift store. He didn't need any reminders of Indigo Springs when he was gone.

The steps ended at a cheerfully decorated country kitchen that smelled of freshly baked chocolate chip cookies. A plate of them sat on the counter near where Aunt Felicia stood between two rows of white cabinets. She hadn't yet changed from the blue dress she'd worn to church.

"Did you find everything?" She wrung her

hands, betraying her uneasiness. They'd barely exchanged two sentences when he'd arrived before he asked about his unwanted belongings and she directed him to the basement.

"I've got it all unless there's more than one box."

"No." More hand-twisting. "Just the one."

"Then I'll get out of your way."

"I made cookies after church," she blurted, halting his progress. "Would you like one?"

It was well known his great-aunt liked to bake, but he was surprised she'd come straight home and made the cookies. Maybe she baked something every Sunday. The ultimate homemaker, she seemed to enjoy doing the things that made a house a home.

"Sure," he said, because it seemed rude to refuse. He carried the box to the table and set it down before taking a cookie. He bit into it, the gooey, chocolate taste bringing back one of the rare pleasures of his childhood. "It's good."

She half smiled, the compliment seeming to please her. "How was the wedding?"

"Fine." He finished off the rest of the cookie. "Johnny's a lucky guy."

"I heard…" She stopped, started again. "I heard you didn't stay long."

So the locals were already gossiping about

him. He'd been up most of the night, second-guessing himself for not accepting Sara's invitation. But he'd done the right thing. He couldn't risk having somebody spot him leaving her house at an odd hour.

"I was at the wedding long enough." He noticed the handle of a cabinet door was loose and thought about offering to fix it, then changed his mind, knowing that would only prolong a visit that was becoming increasingly uncomfortable. "I should get going."

Aunt Felicia finally moved, only to cut off his exit from the kitchen. "Could you, um, look at something for me first?"

The loose handle?

"All right," he said.

She picked up a manila envelope from her kitchen table and wordlessly handed it to him. The envelope was stamped Registered Mail and contained the return address of a local Indigo Springs bank. The first paper he pulled out was a Notice of Intent to Foreclose. A letter stated that Aunt Felicia was several months behind on her loan payments.

He flipped through the papers, trying to make sense of them. The house should be paid off. Aunt Felicia had inherited it when her parents died, and that had probably been twenty-five years ago.

His head jerked up. "It says here you took out a home equity loan."

"I didn't," she said miserably. "Murray must have. I trusted he knew best about money matters. When he'd tell me to sign something, I would."

Michael didn't need to ask why Murray needed money. Even as a teenager, he'd been aware of her late husband's gambling problem. And the bastard had put up Aunt Felicia's house as collateral to finance it.

"I didn't know about the loan until I got the letter," Aunt Felicia explained. "It says the mortgage statements were going to a post office box."

"You've been doing business at this bank for years. Why didn't somebody tell you about this sooner?"

"They're all strangers now. Even Quincy retired about a year ago." She hugged herself. "I don't know what to do. I didn't even know Murray had a post office box."

Michael swallowed his anger. Railing about her no-good late husband wouldn't do Aunt Felicia any good. If he was going to help her, he needed to keep a level head. "When did you get this notice?"

"Friday," she said.

"It says the entire mortgage is due in thirty

days and if you don't pay the amount, you're in default. Can you cover it?"

She shook her head, her expression strained. "I used my savings for funeral expenses."

"Didn't Murray have life insurance?"

"He cashed in the policy before he died." She blinked as though to keep from crying. "I'm going to lose my home, aren't I?"

Michael wished he could pay off the money his aunt owed, but the Peace Corps didn't pay a salary, just a stipend covering basic necessities. His meager bank balance reflected that reality. But lose her house? Not if he could help it.

"You should go to the bank Monday morning and try to straighten this out," he advised.

"I already called the bank." She sniffled. "They said I waited too long for them to help me."

"Then you can hire a lawyer who knows foreclosure law." He dredged up the name of the attorney who'd once threatened to file a civil suit against him on behalf of Quincy Coleman. "Doesn't Larry Donatelli go to your church?"

"He had a heart attack last year and moved to Florida," his aunt said.

That explained why Sara Brenneman felt as though there was room in town for another lawyer.

Sara. Who'd told him at the wedding that she counted foreclosures as one of her specialties.

"I might know someone," he said.

"Really?" His aunt's blue eyes, so like his own, filled with hope that extinguished almost as soon as it appeared. "But lawyers are expensive."

"I'll help with the fees." Michael could swing that much.

"Oh, no," his aunt said instantly, her back straightening. "I can't let you do that."

"You don't even know what she'll charge. She hasn't opened her practice yet so you'd probably get a good rate." Michael could possibly get Sara to quote his aunt a low hourly fee and let him make up the difference. "It can't hurt to ask."

She worked her bottom lip, deep worry lines appearing on her face and making her look older. "Will you call her for me?"

Too late he remembered Sara was having problems getting her phone service hooked up.

"Her phones aren't working, and she mentioned she'd be out of town today," he said, remembering her shopping trip. "I'll show you where her office is and you can stop by Monday."

He saw her throat constrict as she swallowed. "Will you come with me?"

Self-preservation told him to refuse, but in truth he'd decided to help her as soon as he'd seen the foreclosure notice. She hadn't stopped her husband from kicking him out when he turned eighteen, but she had housed and fed him for almost three years. He couldn't let her lose the house.

Even if it meant seeing Sara again and being reminded of what he couldn't have.

"I'll be by tomorrow morning at about nine." He lifted the box from the table.

"Wait." The relief on her face mixed with confusion. "Where are you going?"

"Back to the hotel."

"You can stay here," she said. "In your old room."

Trying to figure out whether the invitation was sincere, he shifted the box in his arms. It wasn't heavy, but it was an awkward shape. "I'll still help you if I stay in a hotel tonight."

"But it makes no sense for you to go to a hotel."

Yet she hadn't even opened the door to him Friday night. He didn't voice his reservation, but it must have been obvious.

"I can explain about Friday night." Her lower lip trembled. "I would have asked you in, but my bridge group was here."

"I understand," he said, his voice monotone.

"No, you don't," she said. "Jill Coleman's in my group."

Jill Coleman. Quincy's wife. Chrissy's mother.

"I thought it would be…" She stopped, searched for a word. "…awkward."

He almost asked her awkward for whom, but he wouldn't like the answer. He started to refuse her invitation, but the prospect of another night in a hotel depressed him.

Besides, there was plenty at his aunt's house to keep him occupied. The loose handle on the cabinet door, for starters.

"I'll put this box in the car and be back with my bag," he said. "You don't need to show me the room. I remember where it is."

CHAPTER FOUR

BECAUSE OF a cardboard bakery box, Laurie Grieb decided returning to Indigo Springs might have been a mistake.

Not because of the apple turnover that was surely inside the small container, but because her resolve to refuse the delicious treat was wavering.

"C'mon, Laurie," drawled the man holding out the dessert. *Like Adam extending the apple to Eve,* Laurie thought. It was after nine o'clock Monday morning and they were in the driveway of her mother's house, which Laurie had moved back into a week ago. "We both know you love apple turnovers."

He spoke in the same cajoling tone he'd once used to get her to make love with him when she was a teenager. Even though her resulting pregnancy had taught her how important it was to resist him, she grabbed the box.

"Okay, fine." Her mouth watered at the sugary-sweet smell drifting up from the box. "But I'm only taking it because I skipped breakfast. It doesn't mean I want you coming around, Kenny."

"You're welcome." He managed to inject a touch of vulnerability in his slight smile.

She felt about two feet tall until she remembered the reasons she couldn't let Kenny Grieb back into her life. His dark sunglasses illustrated one of them. She guessed he wore them more to conceal bloodshot eyes than as a shield from the sun. The Kenny she'd known wasn't so much a big drinker as a reckless one, but then irresponsibility was the theme of his life. Too bad she hadn't figured that out until she'd married him.

"You're hungover."

"You're right. Say the word, and I'll stop drinking. I've done it for you before."

She closed her eyes at the pain that pierced through her at his casual remark. He'd stopped drinking when she was pregnant. Though her pregnancy, the reason he'd married her, had only lasted four months.

"I don't want you to do anything for me." She kept her tone clipped so he wouldn't know she was touched by his gesture. "I mean it, Kenny. Leave me alone. No more turnovers. No more flowers. No more phone calls."

"Now is that any way to talk to your husband?"

"Ex-husband," she corrected sharply. "We've been divorced for seven years."

They'd gotten married straight out of high-school almost nine years ago and hadn't even managed to make their marriage last two years.

"A mistake." He'd gained weight since they'd been together, but not enough to keep him from looking good. His brown hair was the length she liked, long enough that the ends curled and clipped the collar of the green T-shirt he wore with khaki shorts. "I never should have let you go."

"You married somebody else six months later!"

"Another mistake," he said.

That, at least, was the truth. His second marriage, to a singer who performed on the Pennsylvania pub circuit, had lasted only weeks. She'd heard they'd eloped after a quick court-ship. Kenny was good at giving women the rush.

"I don't have time to stand out here listening to you, Kenny. I have things to do." She walked past him to the compact car parked in the driveway, careful to avoid physical contact.

"Where you going?" he asked.

"I have a job interview at nine-thirty." Now why had she told him that? She didn't owe Kenny a single thing, not even answers. She gazed at him meaningfully over the roof of her car. "Speaking of jobs, don't you have one?"

"Sure do," he said. "But Annie said I could take the eleven o'clock trip today."

Annie Sublinski owned Indigo River Rafters. So that was the reason he was dressed in shorts and a T-shirt with the Indigo River Rafters logo rather than in his mechanic's overalls. "What happened to your job at the auto shop?"

He didn't reply, providing her with the answer. "You got fired, didn't you?"

"I decided to go in a different direction."

She should show Kenny it didn't make one iota of difference what he did by getting in her car and driving away. Instead she quirked an eyebrow. "Oh, really? And what direction is that?"

He seemed to be groping for an answer, but her patience had run out. She yanked open the car door. "Never mind. Forget I asked."

"Wait," he said. Like an idiot, she did. "What kind of job are you interviewing for?"

"A receptionist. At a law firm." Why, oh why, had she answered him? Why couldn't she just get in the car and drive away?

The space between his eyebrows narrowed. "Is the lawyer's name Sara Brenneman?"

That stopped her from stepping into the car. "Yeah. Why? Do you know her?"

His mouth twisted. "She was at Johnny Pollock's wedding with Michael Donahue."

He snarled the last name, telling Laurie all she needed to know. The years hadn't dulled his hatred for the man Chrissy Coleman had chosen over him.

"Goodbye, Kenny." Laurie finally found the strength to get in the car and slam the door.

Kenny Grieb was an irresponsible lout, enough reason not to let him back into her life, but not the main reason.

No. The main reason she'd never again give Kenny her heart was that he hadn't gotten his back from a dead woman.

"YOU NEVER had any intention of hiring me!" The young woman Sara was interviewing for the position of office manager leaped to her feet, pointing an accusatory finger at Sara. "It's because you heard I was pregnant, isn't it?"

"Of course not," Sara responded while she wondered what else could go wrong this morning.

First her alarm clock had blared just as Michael Donahue was pulling her into his arms, driving home the frustrating fact they'd never get together outside her dreams.

Then her cell phone had rung with nothing but bad news. The phone company couldn't send someone over until tomorrow, and the contractor she'd hired to paint the interior of her office couldn't come at all.

And now this.

"Don't you give me that!" the woman railed, her robust anger infusing her face with color and making her hair seem redder. "I know everybody in this shit hole of a town has been gossiping about me and Chase."

By Chase, she must mean Chase Bradford, the best man at Johnny Pollock's wedding. Now that the connection had been pointed out to her, Sara remembered where she'd seen the woman before—at the wedding, complaining to Chase that he was neglecting her. That was after Penelope had mentioned Chase's girlfriend was pregnant.

But that was all the prior information Sara had had about Mandy Smith, the first of two women who'd responded to her ad for an office manager. Although Sara had specified applicants should e-mail her a résumé before their appointment, Mandy hadn't provided one.

"You're out of line, Ms. Smith," Sara said, carefully keeping her own anger in check.

"Me? What about you? You're the one who says I'm lying about being a receptionist!"

Sara gritted her teeth. "I said I needed to check your references."

"Just forget it!" The woman was shouting now, although Sara wasn't exactly sure why. "I wouldn't work here if you begged me."

She turned on her heel and stalked away, yanking open the door just as a brunette about Sara's age was preparing to enter.

"If you're here for an interview, don't bother," Mandy bit out. "You won't like the boss."

Mandy brushed past the new arrival, who looked at Sara and made a comical face. Dressed in a suit so red it assaulted the eyes, the woman had an open, friendly face and wildly curling brown hair. "Are you the boss I won't like? You look okay to me but I could be missing something. You don't have horns, do you?"

Sara's heart rate, which had elevated during the confrontation, began to slow. This was a woman she could like. "They're retractable."

The woman's laugh started low in her throat and rumbled outward, an infectious sound.

"I'm Laurie, your nine-thirty appointment." She tried to smooth her hair down but it bounced back into place. "Sorry about the crazy hair. I wanted to make a good impression but the wind got hold of it and poof, there it curled."

Sara couldn't help but smile. She held out a hand. "Sara Brenneman."

Laurie took it without hesitation, grasping her hand firmly and squeezing gently while meeting her eyes. When she let go, she said, "So. What was that woman's deal?"

"I'm not sure, but I'm having my share of headaches today." Sara gestured at the chipped, dingy walls around them. "I'm trying to have the office ready by next Monday, but the painter I hired canceled because he was double-booked."

"Not a problem," Laurie said. "I'll get you some quotes from other painters. Should I get started on that?"

"Ye…" Sara stopped in mid agreement. "Wait a minute. I haven't even interviewed you yet."

Laurie's dark eyes twinkled. "You can't blame a girl for trying. You'd be making a mistake not to hire me. I'm likeable. I'm experienced. And I'm up for anything."

"Then let's get you interviewed." Sara settled into the chair behind the unusually shaped reception desk while Laurie made a fuss over it. Without being told, Laurie pulled a chair up to the desk. Sara riffled through her briefcase until she found the completed application Laurie had e-mailed last week and which Sara hadn't looked at since.

"Let's see." Sara blanched, blinked, then double-checked the name on the application. She'd read it right the first time: Laurie Grieb. She tried to sound as casual as possible when she asked, "Are you, by any chance, related to Kenny Grieb?"

"You know Kenny?"

"Not really." Sara wasn't sure how to raise the subject or even whether she should. Considering Kenny Grieb's actions at the wedding, though, she needed all the details in order to decide whether to employ one of his relatives. "I, um, was with someone at a wedding Saturday who had a minor altercation with him."

"You mean Kenny picked a fight?" Tension radiated off her, like a blast of heat from a wild fire. "Was he drunk?"

"Very."

"Who was the fight with?" Laurie's body stiffened, as though she was bracing herself for the answer.

Sara couldn't think of a reason not to tell her. In fact, this could be her chance to find out why people at the wedding were whispering about his return. "Michael Donahue."

"Damn it!" Laurie expelled a long breath. Before Sara could ask for specifics on Michael, Laurie pulled herself together and let loose with another spate of words. "I'm sorry. I didn't answer your question yet. Kenny's my ex-husband. It's been over between us for a long time, pretty much since I miscarried the baby I was pregnant with when he married me."

It didn't seem over to Sara, a sentiment that must have shown on her face.

"It *is* over. It's just that Kenny stopped by this morning to bring me an apple turnover, which he knows is a weakness of mine, and fed me a load of bull." She stopped, clasped her hands together and rolled her eyes. "Listen to me, going on like this at a job interview. A job that, incidentally, I would be perfect for. If I can ever get you to believe I'm not a lunatic."

Sara laughed, charmed by Laurie despite her connection to Kenny Grieb. But then, she'd been sold on Laurie since she'd asked if Sara had horns. "I don't think you're a lunatic. Free-spirited, yes, but not insane."

"Good, because I'm a terrific office manager and I'm great on the phone. Just call Buddy—he was my boss at the brokerage firm where I worked in Atlanta—and he'll vouch for me."

"Why did you leave Atlanta?"

"I got homesick," she said. "Also, I got to thinking my mom won't be around forever. My dad died fifteen years ago. Mom's not even sixty but…" She trailed off suddenly. "I'm talking too much, aren't I?"

"Not at all," Sara said.

"Then how am I doing?"

Sara smiled. She couldn't imagine Laurie blending in at the stuffy law practice Sara had left behind in Washington, D.C., but the woman with the crazy hair would fit perfectly into the new life Sara was building. "You're hired."

Laurie's eyes bugged out. "Without checking references?"

In hindsight that didn't seem like the smartest idea, even though Sara's impulse was to trust her intuition. She settled on a compromise. "I should have said you're hired if your references check out."

"Me and my big mouth," Laurie groused, then brightened. "They'll check out. So should I start calling around to find a new painting contractor? Lots of people say they won't give ballpark estimates over the phone, but I'll talk them into it. Give me twenty minutes. Tops."

It took fifteen, after which Sara sent Laurie home with a promise to call her although they both knew the decision had already been made.

When she was alone, Sara frowned over the estimates Laurie had gathered. She was missing only one, from a contractor Laurie hadn't been able to talk into giving her one on the phone. Of the other quotes, the highest came from the only painter who could do the job this week. The lowest was twice as much as the original contractor had cited.

Sara would be tempted to do the job herself if it didn't involve dry wall repair, because money was quickly becoming an issue. She'd used most of her savings to buy the row house, which had come "as-is," and then realized she'd underestimated start-up costs for a new business.

She was half tempted to go back to bed, pull the covers over her head to block out the sun and escape into her dream world with Michael Donahue.

Michael Donahue, whom she hadn't asked Laurie about. No matter. He'd walked out of her life without a second glance and she needed to stop thinking about him.

She jerked her head up at the sound of the front door opening, expecting to see a man in paint-splattered overalls. Instead, clutching a manila envelope, a small woman who looked to be in her mid-seventies entered the office, followed by…

"Michael!" It was as if her thoughts had

conjured him up. More than a head taller than the woman, he wore khaki pants and a loose-fitting short-sleeved shirt he'd probably bought to help him withstand the heat of Niger. Sunlight streamed into the office, illuminating the handsome planes and angles of his face and his fading bruise. "I thought you left town."

"Hello, Sara." His eyes fastened on her face and a memory of the kiss assailed her. "I had a change of plans."

Her mind raced with possibilities. Was she the reason he'd changed his mind about staying in town? Had he thought about her even a fraction as much as she'd thought about him?

"Aunt Felicia, this is Sara Brenneman, the attorney I was telling you about," he said. "Sara, this is my great-aunt, Felicia Feldman."

Sara knew so little about Michael, she hadn't been aware he had a great-aunt. Calling upon her professionalism, she got to her feet and came across the room intending to shake hands with the older woman. Instead of a hand, Mrs. Feldman held out the manila envelope.

"Michael said you might look at this for me." Her voice shook even more than her hands, lending her an air of frailty. "It's a foreclosure notice. He said you could tell us if there's anything I can do about it."

The reason for Michael's reappearance slammed through Sara, and disappointment rushed through her like the white water of a river rapid. Michael's visit wasn't personal, it was business.

"I hope it's okay that we came by," Michael said. "I tried calling but your phones still aren't working."

"It's fine," Sara said, cheering herself with the fact that Michael had thought to come to her.

"The bank's going to foreclose if Aunt Felicia doesn't pay what she owes," Michael said. "Unfortunately she didn't know the loan was in default because the bills were coming to her husband's P.O. box. He died three months ago."

His aunt stood at his side, looking miserable. With foreclosures on the rise across the nation, the desperation emanating from her was something Sara had encountered before. She opened the envelope and took out the Notice of Intent to Foreclose, which seemed harsh under the circumstances.

"In my experience—"

The door opened again, this time admitting a heavyset man with a clipboard. From the smears of paint on his jeans, he could only be the contractor.

"I'm from Lehigh Painting," he announced in a gruff, hurried voice. "You need the entire downstairs painted, right?"

"Right." Sara was about to tell him to show himself around, but he'd already disappeared into the back of the office.

"Sorry about the interruption. I was about to say lenders don't want to foreclose because it costs them money in the long run. Taxes. Broker fees. Property maintenance until they can sell." Sara noted from the letterhead that the bank was independent and locally owned. "So they're usually open to working something out. Have you contacted the bank yet, Mrs. Feldman?"

"They said it was too late to do anything," Mrs. Feldman said, twisting her hands.

"Who said that? A loan officer?"

"I think that's what he was."

"It would be better to deal with the branch manager or even the bank president." Sara put the notice back in the envelope. "I can give the bank a call, if you like, and set up a meeting. We can try to get them to refinance the loan. If that doesn't work out, we'll try to get a loan from another institution."

"I still might not be able to afford the payments," Mrs. Feldman said unhappily.

Michael put his hand on his aunt's back. The comforting gesture wasn't directed at her, but Sara's heart melted a little.

"We'll worry about that later," Michael told her. "I'm sure Sara's had experience with cases like yours."

"I have, but I should admit I'm not yet up to speed on Pennsylvania law," Sara said. "I'd have to do some research first, but I'm willing to help if you still want me to."

"Sounds good to me," Michael said.

"Wait." Mrs. Feldman blinked a few times, unshed tears glistening in her eyes. "I need to know how much it will cost."

Because of Mrs. Feldman's dire circumstances, Sara quoted an hourly rate well below what was fair. The woman's face still blanched. Michael must have noticed because he quickly said, "I'll take care of it, Aunt Felicia."

"No," she said forcefully, then continued in a softer, shakier voice. "I can't let you do that, Michael. Not after the way… I just can't let you."

Sara wondered at the source of the guilt written plainly on Mrs. Feldman's face, but it was just one more unknown in the mystery of Michael Donahue.

"I've got that estimate for you." The contractor appeared from the back of the office, handing

Sara a piece of paper. The quote was as distressingly high as the other estimates. "We could fit you in late next week."

"But I need the work finished by Monday," Sara said.

"Impossible. Summer's our busy season. Give us a call, but don't wait too long." He headed out the door without a goodbye, leaving Sara staring after him.

"I swear if I didn't need that drywall repaired, I'd paint the office myself," Sara muttered under her breath.

"I'll do it," Michael offered. "I know my way around drywall and I've done my fair share of painting. If you help out my aunt, I won't charge for labor."

"I thought you were leaving town," Sara said.

"Not until this problem of my aunt's is solved," he said. "So what do you say?"

Sara didn't need to think about it long. "Yes."

"No, Michael," Mrs. Feldman interjected. "I can't ask you to do that for me."

"You didn't ask. I offered." He was putting a spin on his proposal so his aunt would accept his help, Sara realized, wondering at the strain she picked up between them.

Mrs. Feldman chewed her lower lip, appearing unsure whether to accept even though the prospect of losing her home had to be a powerful motivator. "So what can I do for you?"

"You don't have to do anything for me," Michael replied.

"How about if I make you a strawberry pie tonight? That was always your favorite. I'll make roast beef and those mashed potatoes you like, too." She turned to Sara. "Why don't you have dinner with us, Sara?"

"I wouldn't want to intrude," Sara said, fighting the urge to accept.

"You wouldn't be intruding," Michael said so quickly Sara suspected he didn't want to have dinner alone with his aunt. "Please come, Sara."

"Thank you," she said, ignoring her suspicion in favor of believing Michael wanted to have dinner with her. "I will."

QUINCY COLEMAN sat at his usual booth at Jimmy's Diner on Monday morning and ordered a breakfast of an egg-white omelet, whole wheat toast and fresh melon slices. He skipped the coffee for orange juice, a much healthier option.

"How long you been ordering the same thing, Quincy?" Ellie Marson tore the top sheet from her order pad, regarding him with one hand on her hip. Her hair had yet to gray and her energy was high, but she'd probably gained twenty pounds in the past twenty years. Quincy prided himself on weighing the same.

"About as long as you've been taking my order, Ellie," Quincy said.

She laughed her raspy smoker's laugh. "That may be, but I still start work at six and you've been getting here later and later. The crowd you used to eat with left an hour ago."

The diner, in fact, was nearly deserted except for a young couple with kids and a pair of hiker types. Probably tourists. The hands on the clock above the counter were inching past ten-thirty, too soon for the lunch crowd.

"You're jealous because you get up early to come to work, and I can sleep in and take my morning hike before you stop serving breakfast," Quincy said.

"You got that right." Ellie headed off to the back of the restaurant, barking an order to the cook as she went.

Quincy caught his reflection in the mirror behind the counter. With his trim build and the suit jacket he always wore when he came into town, he looked damned good for a sixty-six-year-old man.

Appearances, he'd always stressed to his family, were important.

He wouldn't let anyone guess how miserable he'd been since he'd retired as the president of Indigo Springs Bank a year ago. He'd been unhappy before then, too, but his demanding job had occupied his mind. He still served on the bank's board of directors, but now there were too many hours in the day to think about what he'd lost.

His beautiful daughter Chrissy, who'd died before she had a chance to really live.

And his wife Jill, who'd walked out on their marriage shortly after Chrissy died.

He rubbed at his eyes, wiping away tears before they had a chance to fall. Ellie returned with his breakfast so quickly the cook must have started his order as soon as Quincy arrived. She put the steaming plate of food in front of him, and he breathed in the scent of egg and toast.

Ellie cocked a hand on one rounded hip. "I suppose you heard Michael Donahue was at Johnny Pollock's wedding?"

"I did." He controlled his temper and offered Ellie the same response he'd given the four people who'd phoned him with the news. "It's a free country. I can't stop him from coming where he's not wanted. I'm just glad he's gone."

"He's not gone," Ellie refuted. "I had a

customer this morning who saw him and his aunt go into that new lawyer's office on Main Street."

"He can't be meaning to stay!" The words erupted from Quincy like lava from a volcano. The family of tourists stopped eating and stared at him.

"Whoa! Don't shoot the messenger. Just passing on what I heard." She backed away from the table, stopping to check on the nosy tourists on the way to the kitchen, leaving Quincy alone with his thoughts.

His turbulent, roiling thoughts.

Michael Donahue was still in town.

Michael Donahue, who'd as good as signed Chrissy's death warrant when he stole her away from Indigo Springs.

Hatred flamed inside Quincy, hotter than fire.

Donahue should never have come back. Quincy would make him wish he'd stayed away.

CHAPTER FIVE

THE ROAST BEEF was tender, the home-style gravy and mashed potatoes delectable and the strawberry pie transcendent, but Michael had never been more eager for a meal to end.

His great-aunt obviously felt the same way. She rose from the sturdy white table in her brightly decorated kitchen to clear their dessert dishes even though Sara had another bite of pie left.

"Thank you for the delicious meal, Mrs. Feldman." Sara was still holding her fork. Michael thought she'd been about to stab the last morsel of pie when his aunt took her plate away. "Let me help you clean up."

"Oh, no. You're a guest." Aunt Felicia couldn't have sounded more horrified if Sara had proposed tossing the dirty dishes in the trash. "It's such a nice night. You and Michael go sit on the porch."

It sounded more like an order than a request, which Michael supposed it was, one he was glad to obey. When they were outside, he sat down on his aunt's pine swing, which hung from large hooks screwed into the porch ceiling, and rolled his shoulders, wishing away the tension.

Sara sat down next to him, running her fingers over the smooth hardwood of the armrest. Tonight she looked beautiful in a sleeveless crinkled cotton dress in khaki green, but Michael had already figured out she'd look striking no matter what she wore.

"I'm going to buy one of these swings for my deck," she said. "Then I'll stock up on mint juleps, never mind that this is the north. Mint juleps just seem like something you should drink while sitting on a porch swing. Don't look at me like that."

She slapped him lightly on the arm, her smile charmingly embarrassed. He couldn't help smiling back. Something about her—hell, *everything* about her—lifted his spirits higher than they'd been in years. "Like what?"

"Like I'm…corny," she supplied. "But I guess I can't expect you to understand, with you not being a porch-swing kind of guy."

"I don't know about that. I spent a lot of time

on this very swing." He scuffed his foot against the wood floor, sending the swing rocking. "I used to come out here at night, turn off the light and just swing and swing."

"So this isn't the first time your aunt chased you out here?" Sara asked rhetorically. "Um, did I say something wrong tonight?"

He decided to be honest. "You asked too many questions."

"What? How is asking Felicia whether she grew up in Indigo Springs and when she got married asking too many questions?"

Aunt Felicia had initially been forthcoming, telling Sara about being raised in this very house, about Murray moving in after they got married, about staying on after her parents died.

It was all good information, allowing Sara to understand how much the house meant to her. The manager of the Indigo Springs Bank was on vacation until Friday, but Sara was now determined to fight harder at the meeting she'd scheduled to make sure his aunt kept her home.

"Those questions weren't the problem," Michael said. "She didn't want to talk about me."

Aunt Felicia had clammed up after Sara asked about how she and Michael were related. Surely Sara had noticed. She'd revealed that her late sister was Michael's grandmother, then shut up.

"Why didn't she want to talk about you?" Sara asked.

He let the swing rock back and forth until it came to a stop. Sara had been fishing for answers since he'd met her, and it was time he provided some of them.

"I moved in with her after my mother died. I was sixteen but I'd only met her once, when she came to visit us in Florida. It was pretty obvious from the start that my being here was making trouble for her."

"Trouble? How?"

"Aunt Felicia's husband didn't want me living with them."

"You mean your uncle?"

"I never thought of him as my uncle, and he sure didn't treat me like a nephew. The day I turned eighteen, he told me to leave."

Her mouth dropped open. "Whatever for?"

"He said he didn't need a reason." He recited what he remembered of Murray's speech without emotion. When it came to Murray, he'd never been emotional. "An eighteen year old was an adult and should be able to fend for himself."

"That's really callous." Her voice was full of empathy. "What did your aunt say?"

Ah, his aunt. She was the one who'd mattered. "She said she was sorry."

Sara placed a hand on his arm. In the light from the porch he could see her eyes were soft with compassion for the boy he'd been. "Now I understand why you and your aunt are uncomfortable around each other."

"So you noticed?" He kept his voice light. Just barely. His aunt never forgot to send cards at Christmas and on his birthday, but that was the extent of her interest in him. "Before last weekend, I hadn't seen her since I left town."

"Is that what you did after Murray kicked you out? Left town?"

"Not right away," he said. "The Pollocks took me in. Mr. Pollock even gave me a job. I already knew, though, that I wouldn't stick around for long."

"Where did you go when you left Indigo Springs?"

Tell her, Michael thought. *Tell her you didn't leave alone.*

But that wasn't what she had asked.

"Johnstown. It's a couple of hundred miles west of here. I went to community college at night and worked construction during the day."

Everything he told her was true, but vastly misleading at the same time because he was leaving out so much.

Chrissy leaving Indigo Springs with him.

Chrissy growing increasingly unhappy away from everything she'd ever known.

Chrissy dying.

It was a miracle somebody in town hadn't told her about it before now. That left it up to him to tell her.

Right now.

Except Sara leaned over and kissed him. Her fingers spiked through his hair, cradling his scalp, holding his head in place so she could fasten her mouth more securely to his.

He'd been trying not to think about the last time she'd kissed him, but this kiss brought the feelings she'd stirred up bursting to the surface.

He might have fooled himself into believing he'd stayed in town only because of his aunt, but that wasn't true.

The more compelling reason was in his arms.

She tasted of the strawberries from his aunt's pie, but he'd sampled her kisses before and knew they'd always be sweet.

She parted her lips, and he accepted her silent invitation, deepening the kiss with an erotic slide of tongue on tongue. His body hardened, his erection straining against the denim of his jeans.

A phone rang inside the house, a jarring reminder that they were on a lighted porch where anybody who happened to be passing by could see them, but he couldn't seem to stop kissing her, as though she were a drug of which he couldn't get enough.

"Michael." His aunt's voice followed by the creak of the screen door finally gave him the resolve he needed to break the kiss.

Sara's eyes were closed, appropriate because she didn't know exactly who it was she'd been kissing.

"Oh. Excuse me." Aunt Felicia took one look at them and backed away. "I didn't know… I shouldn't have…"

"It's okay, Aunt Felicia." Michael was pleased with the even tone of his voice, especially since he didn't feel in control at all. Sara edged away from him, but only slightly. "What is it?"

"The phone…" Her voice trailed off again.

"What about the phone?" Michael prodded as gently as he could, hiding his frustration. Not so much at the interruption as his own inability to put a halt to the kiss. "Who was it?"

"He didn't say." She seemed reluctant to continue. "He said…he said I should tell you that you should never have come back."

"Well, of all the nerve." Sara fumed, the first thing she'd said since the kiss. "Did you check caller ID?"

"I don't have caller ID," Aunt Felicia said. "And I didn't recognize the voice."

"Anybody cowardly enough not to identify himself doesn't deserve to be listened to." Sara sounded like the lawyer she was, confident and sure of herself. "Just forget he ever called."

"That's not all," Aunt Felicia ventured. "He said Michael should check his car."

Michael was out of the swing almost before she finished the sentence, striding down the steps and to the curb where he'd parked the PT Cruiser. The rental was between street lamps, more in shadow than in light. Something about the car seemed off-kilter. As he neared, he realized the reason. The body of the car sat much lower to the street than it should.

"Somebody slashed your tires!" Sara ran ahead of him to the car. "Can you believe it? Who would do something like this?"

Michael could come up with a dozen candidates, with Kenny Grieb topping the list. There weren't many people in town who wouldn't think he had worse things coming to him than slashed tires.

"Well, they're not getting away with it." Sara pulled a razor-thin cell phone from the deep pocket of her dress and flipped up the cover.

Michael closed his hands over hers. "What are you doing?"

"Calling the police."

"No."

"No?" Even though it was dark, he could see white all around her pupils. "Why not?"

"Because I'll take care of it. My rental insurance should cover the damage."

"Somebody deliberately slashed your tires!" She said the words slowly as though he didn't grasp the full import of what had happened.

He had a much better idea than she did.

"It's not worth making a big deal over," he said.

"It is if the vandal's still out there slashing somebody else's tires!"

Michael walked to the Volkswagen parked behind the PT Cruiser, verifying its tires were fine. So, too, were the tires on the Chevy across the street. "It's only my car."

"You can't possibly know that!"

But he did. He'd have known it without the anonymous call. "Drop it, Sara."

"This is something that should be reported, not dropped. It doesn't matter if you're the only one who had his tires slashed. It's a crime, and criminals should suffer consequences."

She sounded like a lawyer in a courtroom fighting for truth, justice and the American way.

A lawyer without all the facts. She got her phone in position to dial again.

"I said butt out, Sara," he said tightly. "It's not your problem. Not your business."

His harsh words sliced through the night. She recoiled. A weaker woman might have surrendered to tears, but a blankness descended over Sara's face.

"I need to be going." The warmth was gone from her voice, something that Michael could only blame on himself. "Please thank your aunt again for dinner."

"I'll walk you to your car," Michael offered.

"No need for that. Good-night." She walked stiffly away, obviously angry.

He smothered the urge to chase her and explain, but it was best she didn't get involved with his problems. And she wouldn't, if he could stay away from her for four more days. With any luck, his aunt's trouble would be over after that meeting at the bank on Friday.

Now all he had to figure out was how to keep his distance from a woman he desperately wanted while working downstairs from where she lived.

THE SOLES of Sara's running shoes squeaked as she walked back and forth over the hardwood floors of her office. She'd gotten quite a workout on the hilly three-mile jog she'd taken to start the morning and needed to cool down gradually.

She was not pacing.

She was not nervous about meeting Michael in—she checked her watch—less than fifteen minutes.

She was not going to forgive him for last night simply because she wanted to kiss him again.

After she gave him a key to the downstairs, she'd work from upstairs until he was finished with the job so she didn't have to see him any more than was necessary.

"At least I'm not a complete liar," she muttered aloud. "Because I do want to kiss him again."

Through the open blinds of the window facing the street she spotted a silver-colored Cadillac pulling up to the curb. A small, trim man of about sixty wearing a dark business suit, his gray hair slicked back from an angular, stern face, got out of the car. Then he headed purposefully toward her office.

"Oh, crap." Her hand flew to her ponytail, but taking down her hair wouldn't come close to making herself look presentable.

She plastered on a professional smile when he entered the office, as though she greeted every potential client while wearing gym shorts, a sleeveless tank top and running shoes.

"Hello. I'm Sara Brenneman." She stopped short of offering her hand, but only because she was sure it was damp. "As you can see, I haven't yet officially opened my practice. However, I am available for consultation. Although not, obviously, right now."

He didn't return her smile. Neither did he bother to pull the door shut behind him.

"I'm not here to hire you, young lady," he said gruffly. "I'm here to welcome you to Indigo Springs."

He didn't sound very welcoming.

"Thank you," she said.

"I'm Quincy Coleman."

Quincy Coleman. She'd heard his name before, it seemed in relation to Michael. Yes, that was right. The men she'd overheard outside the church had been speculating about what Coleman would do when he found out Michael was back in town.

"It's very neighborly of you to come by," she said.

He stood statue-still, his body between her and the open door so he blotted out the sunlight. "Indigo Springs is overrun with tourists in the summer, but it's still the kind of place where neighbors look out for neighbors."

His words should have sounded kind, but they had a hard, unpleasant edge.

"That's one reason I moved here," Sara said.

"Good to hear, because I've got a *friendly* piece of advice." His angry eyes bored into hers. "If you want to be successful in this town, stay away from Michael Donahue."

"Excuse me?" She'd sensed he was driving at something unpleasant, had even guessed it involved Michael, but could never have anticipated the stark hatred emanating from him.

"Everybody knows you were with Donahue at Johnny Pollock's wedding and that you were at his aunt's house last night."

Her spine stiffened. "I don't see how that's any of your business."

"People will give you the benefit of doubt since you're new in town," he continued, as though he hadn't heard her. "They'll figure you didn't know what he was, but that'll only last so long."

His manner was so presumptuous she should have asked him to leave, but curiosity stopped her. Michael's certainty that last night's vandal had targeted only him made Sara feel she was missing half the story.

"What do you mean?" she asked. "What don't I know?"

"He didn't tell you, did he?"

"Tell me what?"

"That he's a murderer." Coleman's features

twisted with disgust so tangible she felt as though it was spewing from him.

Sara backed away, unwilling to get sprayed.

"I don't believe you," she said.

Michael was a hero. She'd seen him rescue that little boy from certain death with her own eyes.

His discordant laugh was without mirth. "What is it about Donahue that makes it so easy for him to manipulate women? Is it his handsome face?"

"If you knew me," she said tightly, "you'd realize I'm not easy to manipulate."

"Yet here you are defending a murderer."

"I'm defending a man I know to be a good man," she said.

"Does a good man talk a girl into dropping out of high-school and leaving town with him in the middle of the night? Does a good man promise to marry her and then lie to her and cheat on her?" The tone of his voice escalated with every question. "Does a good man get so angry when she tries to leave him that he drags her out of a bar, says she's coming home with him and speeds down a narrow back road?"

Sara started to get a sick feeling in her stomach. She should ask him to leave, tell him she didn't want to hear any more, but couldn't form any words.

"That girl was my daughter, Chrissy," Coleman continued. "She was in the passenger seat the night your 'good man' lost control of the car. The car left the road and rolled down an embankment before it slammed into a tree. Neither of them was wearing a seat belt. They were both ejected. Donahue lived. My daughter died."

Sara could barely process the information. His story didn't seem to leave much room for interpretation except there had to be more to it than what he was telling.

"But—" she began.

"Don't you dare make excuses for him," he retorted. "Chrissy was only eighteen when she died. Eighteen!"

Sara had thought Quincy Coleman nondescript when she'd glimpsed him through the window, the sort of businessman getting on in years she'd passed on the street a dozen times a day when she lived in Washington, D.C. Ordinary. Harmless.

However, the vitriol radiating from the man transformed him, making him look fierce and capable of anything.

"You're the one who slashed the tires on Michael's car," she accused.

"If you keep hanging around him, somebody might slash yours, too."

"Are you threatening me?"

Coleman advanced toward her, the first time he'd moved since entering the office. "I'm advising you to be careful of the company you keep."

"That sounds like a threat to me." Michael stood in the open doorway, giving the same response Sara had been about to make. His voice was low, his body taut. "Your beef is with me. Leave Sara out of it."

Quincy Coleman whirled on Michael, his skin turning red and splotchy. "You brought her into it! Then you didn't even have the guts to tell her you were a murderer!"

Sara waited for Michael to defend himself against the outrageous charge, but he stood rigidly silent.

"What? You've got nothing to say?" Coleman shouted, his breathing harsh and uneven. "Aren't you going to tell her how you got away with murder?"

Coleman looked angry enough to attack, but still Michael said nothing.

"That's enough, Mr. Coleman." Sara positioned herself between the two men, suddenly sure that Michael wouldn't defend himself if Coleman did throw a punch. "I'm going to have to ask you to leave."

"Not until you understand I'm not threatening you," Coleman said. "I'm warning you. Like I wish someone had warned my Chrissy."

"Mr. Coleman," Sara began.

"I'm going." He stalked to the door but turned before he exited, pointing a finger at Michael. "Just don't let yourself be fooled by anything *he* says."

He slammed the door shut behind him, and then for long moments there was absolute silence. The only part of Michael that moved was his jaw, which he was clenching.

"Well?" Sara prompted. "Aren't you going to say something?"

"Like what?"

"Like how unjust it is for Quincy Coleman to go around calling you a murderer! Why, he practically admitted he was the one who slashed your tires!"

The indignation she expected to appear on Michael's face never came. "It crossed my mind he might have done it," he said.

She didn't understand his detached attitude, his quiet acceptance of Coleman's accusations. "Then you should have let me call the police. If I had, maybe he wouldn't be slandering you."

"The truth isn't slander, Sara," Michael said,

sounding tired. "There are things you don't know, things I should have told you before now."

"You can't tell me anything to make me believe Quincy Coleman."

"How about this?" Michael asked. "He's right. His daughter is dead because of me."

"No," she breathed.

"Yes. She left town with me because she thought I loved her. She was wrong."

"You were only eighteen! You'd just been thrown out of your aunt's house. Of course you wanted somebody to care about you."

"Would you stop making excuses for me and listen? Coleman had me arrested for vehicular homicide, but the charges didn't stick. I should have been convicted. I should have gone to jail."

Sara stared at him mutely, trying to process what he was telling her. It was too much, too fast. In the legal arena she prided herself on clear thinking, but she couldn't wrap her mind around any of it.

He expelled an audible breath and ran a hand over his lower face. "I'll understand if you don't want me to paint your office, but please don't drop my aunt's case. I'll pay your usual rate. Just give me the bill and don't let her know how much it really costs."

"Wait a minute." The cluttered thoughts in

her head coalesced into one: He was trying to back out of their business arrangement. "Why wouldn't I want you to paint my office?"

"You heard Coleman. You'll have a hard time getting accepted in this town if you're connected to me."

"I don't care what Coleman said. We had an agreement, and I'm holding you to it."

"Are you sure that's smart?"

With Michael trying hard to convince her that Coleman's accusations had merit, Sara wasn't sure of anything except she'd never been one to let what other people thought dictate her actions.

"I'm sure I want you to keep up your end of the bargain," she said.

Michael didn't speak for long moments, then held some sheets out to her. "I picked up some paint-chip charts. After you choose the colors, I'll buy the paint and get started."

He kept talking, outlining a timetable that would have him finishing the job by the end of the week, but she was only half listening. It was hard to concentrate when she couldn't reconcile her impressions of Michael with what she'd just heard.

If Michael had been driving recklessly that night, Quincy Coleman was right. Michael should have paid for his daughter's life with jail time.

She couldn't help thinking there was more to the story, but how could she continue to defend a man who was so insistent on taking the blame?

CHAPTER SIX

"I've MISSED the hell out of you, Mikey Mike," Johnny Pollock cried later that Tuesday night. "But no way am I letting you win!"

Johnny danced on the balls of his feet across the width of the air hockey table in the noisy arcade, sending shot after shot zinging toward the goal Michael was defending. He looked more like his teenage self than a married man who'd just returned from his honeymoon.

Michael acknowledged his friend's cocky comment with an inelegant snort, even as he positioned his mallet in front of his net and strained to deflect the hard shots.

"Don't want you to let up." Michael had to shout to be heard above the motor of the table's industrial-grade blower combined with the hum of video games. "Victory will be sweeter this way."

"Ha!" Johnny shouted. "You're going down, Donahue!"

Michael took a quick look at the score displayed in glowing red letters on the game's panel. Despite Johnny's relentless attack, they were deadlocked.

He quickly moved his sombrero-shaped mallet to counteract another of Johnny's missiles. The puck ricocheted back to Johnny, who leaned over the table and put all his power into his next shot. The thin black disc was moving at such a high rate of speed that Michael couldn't get his mallet back into position fast enough.

The puck disappeared into Michael's goal, making a clattering sound that meant only one thing.

Game over.

"Got you!" Johnny shouted, pumping a fist.

Michael let go of his mallet and straightened, moving around the table to meet his friend halfway. "What does that make your record against me? Two wins, two-hundred-twenty-two losses?"

"Funny," Johnny said.

"True," Michael countered.

"In this decade, I'm one and oh. That means you owe me a soda."

They maneuvered through the arcade past teens with their eyes riveted to video screens and a skinny, loose-limbed boy navigating a

Dance Dance Revolution video game. Following the directions of an on-screen prompt, the boy duplicated patterns with his quick feet on an arrowed panel.

The arcade led to a brightly lit area featuring a food counter and some booths. A young couple munching hot dogs and French fries occupied a single side of one booth, seated so close together a sheet of paper couldn't fit between them. A trio of boys in another booth scarfed down hamburgers.

"A soda isn't all you owe me," Johnny said after they ordered a couple of root beers.

"Yeah, yeah," Michael said grudgingly. "I remember."

"Well?" Johnny prompted.

"You are the king," Michael stated in a monotone. "All others bow before you."

Johnny laughed uproariously. "I love hearing that!"

"Enjoy it," Michael muttered, "because you might never beat me again."

By mutual silent consent, they carried their drinks outside to a seating area consisting of four picnic tables. None were occupied so they took the one nearest the road and sat side by side facing the street, their legs outstretched.

They'd occupied the same spot years ago, although the old, scarred picnic tables had been replaced with new ones made of recycled plastic. The arcade was busier than it had been back then and so was the section of street in front of it. It used to be that any traffic on a weekday night was rare. Now it looked like a car or two a minute was passing by.

"What's your bride gonna think about you coming home late on your first night back after the honeymoon?" Michael asked.

"Penelope is spending this week fixing up our new place so she'll be cool with it," Johnny said. "Besides, she knows how much I wanted to hang with you. I just never thought you'd be here when I got back."

Michael had already explained that his great-aunt was facing the threat of foreclosure. "Never thought you'd come back so soon."

"According to Penelope, the long weekend in Atlantic City was our pre-honeymoon. The Caribbean cruise this winter is the real deal."

"Can't argue with a woman who wants to get you alone on a boat," Michael said.

"My thoughts exactly." Johnny grinned. "So what's this I hear about you angling to spend another two years with the Peace Corps?"

"You sound surprised."

"I am surprised. I got the feeling you were tired of living in third-world countries."

"Yeah, well, somebody's got to do it."

"You've been doing it for, what, seven years?" Johnny asked.

"Six," Michael corrected. He'd gotten his first assignment at the same time he'd received his community college associate's degree in construction and building management. So far he'd been stationed in Belize, Kenya and Niger.

"It might be time for somebody else to do it," Johnny said.

"I'll be fine once I recharge." The night was warm and the air heavy with humidity. Michael took a swig of root beer, appreciating the sweet taste. He didn't tell Johnny cold soft drinks weren't readily available when you were living in the bush. "I'm thinking about renting a place on a lake after my aunt's situation is squared away."

"Alone?"

"Yeah, alone." Michael directed a sharp look at Johnny. "Who'd be with me?"

"Penelope's friend Sara."

"That's not happening," Michael said quickly.

"Why not?"

"She has to live here after I leave."

"You don't have to leave," Johnny said. "My dad would hire you in a heartbeat. Hell, with your experience, you could start your own company. Or, better yet, form a partnership with us."

Michael started shaking his head before Johnny finished the first sentence. "I can't move back here. I told you about getting my tires slashed. You know how people feel about me."

"I know how *I* feel about you. I know how my dad feels about you."

"Give it a rest, Johnny."

They sat in silence, listening to the whir of tires as the cars passed by. A car horn sounded in the distance. A child squealed with laughter somewhere down the street. Michael remembered it used to be so quiet you could hear the sounds of the arcade through the closed door.

"Know why you used to beat me at air hockey?" Johnny asked.

"Because you stink?"

Johnny usually laughed aloud when Michael made a comment like that, then gave back as good as he'd got. Tonight he didn't even smile.

"Because you never played it safe like you did tonight," Johnny said. "You used to be willing to take a risk."

Michael didn't pretend not to understand that Johnny was talking about more than air hockey. "In some of the countries where I've lived, being an American is taking a risk."

"Yeah, but the Peace Corps sets up where you work, where you live, even who you associate with. That's playing it safe." Johnny stood up, crushing his soda can and tossing it into the waste basket. "For you, taking a risk would be moving back home."

LAURIE SLAMMED the rolled-up newspaper onto the long wooden counter Thursday morning, attracting the attention of every person in the river-rafting shop.

The couple who'd just gotten through prepaying for the next trip down the river stepped back. The man shuffling through a rack of Indigo River Rafters T-shirts looked up. The two young girls trying on men's sunglasses stopped giggling.

But the only person who interested Laurie was working behind the counter.

"Why would you do something like this, Kenny?" Her adrenaline was running so high she had to make a conscious effort not to shout.

"Do what?" Kenny's hazel eyes grew wide and innocent, a trick she remembered from when they were married. It meant he was guilty as hell.

She unrolled the latest edition of a local tabloid and flipped through it. Setting the newspaper down on the counter so it faced Kenny, she jabbed her index finger at a quarter-page display ad at the bottom.

The advertisement looked as if it had been designed by a despondent Cupid. An arrow bisected a heart, splitting it into two sections.

Have pity on my broken heart, read the type embedded in one side of the heart. The message inside the second side was the kicker: *Give me another chance, Laurie.*

There was no signature, but Laurie hadn't questioned who placed the ad for a single second. And to think Kenny had probably arranged for it after picking a fight with Mike Donahue to avenge the dead girl who lived on in his heart.

"So that's what this is about." Kenny actually smiled, revealing the deep dimple on his left cheek she used to think was so sexy. "The ad department did a good job, don't you think?"

"Damn you, Kenny," she snapped. "Don't play dumb with me. I told you to leave me alone and instead you place this stupid ad for everybody in town to see. You know how people talk. Everybody will think we're getting back together."

He tilted his head. They were inside a modified warehouse that housed rafts, tubes, kayaks and paddles while also acting as a retail shop and business office. Morning sunlight spilled through an overhead window, highlighting the golden streaks in Kenny's brown hair. His skin was tanned. Working on the river looked good on him. Damn him.

"Aren't we getting back together?" he asked.

"No!"

He arched both eyebrows. "Then what are you doing here?"

"What kind of question is that? I'm cussing you out, that's what I'm doing."

"You could have picked up the phone. Hell, you could have ignored the ad." He swept one hand in her direction. "Instead, here you are."

She frowned. "So?"

"So you must have wanted to see me."

She mentally reviewed the events that had led her to the river rafters. She'd opened the paper, spotted the ad and stormed out of the house, leaving the cup of coffee she'd been drinking as steamed as she was.

After guessing he'd be at the rafting shop, she'd practically sprinted to the building when she spotted his car in the gravel parking lot.

"Of course I wanted to see you," she said. "How else can I get it through your thick skull that I want you to leave me alone?"

"Think about it, Laurie." He braced both hands on the counter and leaned close. "If you really meant that, you wouldn't only tell me to stay away from you, you'd stay away from me, too."

She jerked backward, temporarily unable to think up a comeback. An attractive woman wearing a green T-shirt identical to Kenny's appeared from the back of the shop and joined Kenny at the counter.

"Hi, Laurie," the woman said with an easy smile. "It's good to see you again."

With a shock, Laurie realized it was Annie Sublinski, a former classmate who'd been so shy when they were in high-school she was like a ghost. If not for the birthmark on the left side of Annie's face, Laurie wouldn't have recognized her even though she knew Annie owned the business.

"Hi, Annie," Laurie said through gritted teeth. If she opened her mouth any wider, she'd start yelling at Kenny again.

Annie's gaze swung from Laurie to Kenny before dipping to the newspaper and coming back up again. "Everything all right?"

"Everything's great," Kenny said. The jerk was actually grinning.

Annie took in the wide-legged navy trousers Laurie wore with a red ballet-neck short-sleeved shirt. "You don't look like you're dressed for rafting, Laurie."

"I'm n-not. I, um…" Laurie stopped, annoyed with herself for stammering. It occurred to her that she and Annie were playing different roles than they had in high school, with all the poise in Annie's corner. "I just came by to tell Kenny something."

"Oh," Annie said as if she understood when she couldn't possibly.

"I've gotta go. I've, um, gotta get t-to work." There she went stammering again, but now she had good reason. The wall clock behind the counter showed it was nearly ten o'clock, the starting time she and Sara had agreed upon for her first official day of work. She hadn't considered she'd be late when she went hunting Kenny.

"I'll be home by five if you feel like doing something," Kenny called after her as she fled. "Just give me a call."

Because she couldn't come up with a snappy reply, she didn't turn around. She just got the hell out of there.

SARA HADN'T been able to go anywhere over the last few days without a friend of Quincy Coleman's warning her to steer clear of Michael.

At the drugstore, it was the gray-haired pharmacist who filled her antihistamine prescription: "Quincy says you can't turn your back on him."

At Jimmy's Diner, the waitress who rang up Sara's takeout order: "I know he's good-looking, but Quincy says a woman can't believe a word he says."

And at the post office, the clerk who sold her stamps: "Quincy says he got away with murder."

Yet here Sara was, standing not six feet from Michael, watching him use a power sander to smooth out a drywall repair.

She wiped her suddenly damp palms on the slim-fitting white pants she wore with a cropped yellow cotton jacket, ignored her jumpy stomach and moved closer to him.

His head swung in her direction, and it seemed to her that the corners of his mouth started to lift. But the glimmer of a smile was gone when he turned off the sander. "Do you need something?"

She needed to see him.

Because no matter what Quincy Coleman said, Michael corroborated and all those friends of Coleman intimated, she didn't believe she'd gotten a true handle on what had happened in Michael's past.

However, she couldn't tell him that.

She held up the letter she'd written the day before announcing the opening of her practice. "I need to get to my copier."

He nodded once, then removed the drop cloth from the copier in a fluid motion and immediately stood back, as though being careful not to get too close to her.

"Thanks," she told him.

He wore an old T-shirt that showed off the definition in his arms and faded jeans that made his legs appear long and rangy. Stubble covered his lower face.

He looked like a conscientious, hard-working man and not the monster Coleman was portraying him to be.

"Anything new on my aunt's case?" he asked.

She was so intent on figuring out a way to get answers that his question threw her. Of course he'd want an update. They had barely seen each other in three days. During the few minutes when she'd approved the paint colors, they'd discussed her choice of a red accent wall in the main lobby but hadn't talked about his aunt at all.

"I've been researching refinancing options, but her best bet is the local bank." She opened the lid of the copier and placed her letter facedown on the glass. "Our appointment's tomorrow morning. I'll hit on her status as a longtime customer, and I hope we'll be able to work something out."

He nodded, his expression that of an impassive stranger. She closed the lid of the copier and pressed the start button but nothing happened. She pressed again, harder this time. Still nothing.

He reached down and picked up one end of an extension cord. Without a word, he plugged it in and the machine whirred to life. She felt her face heat, could almost hear him asking for the real reason she'd interrupted his work.

"Why exactly did the police drop the vehicular homicide charge?" she blurted out.

He stiffened, his eyes becoming even more guarded. *Way to ease into the topic,* she silently berated herself. Now that she'd brought it up, though, she wasn't about to back down. If she did, she'd never get answers.

"You said it was because there wasn't enough evidence, but the forensics teams that reconstruct fatal accidents are good. They can figure out what happened from skid marks."

"There were no skid marks," he said in a monotone.

Her mouth dropped open. It was the last thing she expected him to say. Because in the absence of skid marks, the conclusion was that the driver had made no attempt to stop. That usually only meant one thing.

"Were you drinking that night?" she asked.

"No," he said.

That had to be the truth. The police would have tested his blood alcohol level and detected the presence of any controlled substances. But the driver didn't have to be impaired for charges to stick. The law viewed a vehicle as much of a weapon as a gun. If there weren't skid marks, that alone should have been enough to prove that Michael was driving recklessly.

"Then why did the police drop the charges?" she repeated.

His chest expanded with the deep breath he took. "Because it was an old car and a blind curve. The investigators found a leak in the rear brake line and hardly any fluid in the master cylinder. They couldn't prove the brakes hadn't been bad before the accident."

"But I can't be—"

He didn't let her finish. "It's a matter of record. Look it up if you don't believe it."

"But I—"

He switched on the sander and turned his attention to the wall before she could mount any more protests or ask any more questions.

Realistically, what more could she say? Just because she couldn't envision the Michael of today as a reckless driver didn't mean his nineteen-year-old self was innocent.

People made mistakes, but they grew and changed as the years went by. Take Sara as an example. If she hadn't decided to take a chance on a new life, she'd still be researching case law at that boring law office in Washington, D.C.

I'm warning you. Stay away from Michael Donahue.

She heard Quincy Coleman's voice in her head as she took the copies of her letter from the machine.

You don't know anything about me.

This time she heard Michael's voice, but the flesh-and-blood man was silent, his back to her as he sanded the wall.

She shut both voices out of her mind, focusing instead on the workday ahead. Once Laurie arrived for her first full day, they could start addressing envelopes and calling the phonebook companies to place ads.

First, Sara needed to make sure they had enough caffeine to get through the day.

The coffee was brewing when Laurie knocked on her upstairs door ten minutes past the time they agreed upon. Her color was high, her shirt had come partially loose from her slacks and her hair was even crazier than usual.

"I know I'm late, but I assure you I'm usually very prompt and it won't happen again." Laurie spoke so quickly that her words ran together, blurring the explanation, but she kept talking. "I even forgot what you said about taking that outside staircase to your deck instead of coming in through the office. And I know you mentioned the office was being painted so I should have—"

"Laurie, stop." Sara couldn't let her finish, especially because she suspected the man painting her office was responsible for Laurie's agitation. "Just tell me what's wrong."

Laurie's shoulders sagged and she dropped into the kitchen chair nearest the stairs. "Is it that obvious?"

Sara sat at an angle to her. "Yes. So spill."

"I shouldn't tell you," Laurie said. "You'll think I'm a high-maintenance employee. You might figure I'm too much trouble and fire me before I've even worked here a day."

"I wouldn't have hired you if I was planning to turn around and fire you, so just tell me what happened." Sara braced herself, expecting to hear the name *Michael Donahue,* the way she had all week.

"You must not have seen today's newspaper," Laurie said.

Had somebody announced Michael's return?

"Kenny took out an ad asking for another chance," Laurie continued.

"Kenny?" Sara repeated the name while her mind switched gears. "This isn't about Michael?"

Laurie frowned. "Why would this be about Mike?"

Sara suddenly found it easier to draw air into her lungs. "Never mind. What was in the ad?"

"A broken heart. Can you believe it? When I saw that thing, I got so mad I went tearing out of the house to confront him."

Sara wrinkled her nose. "Not the best way to convince a man you're not interested."

Laurie laid her folded arms on the table and let her head drop onto them. "That's what Kenny said. The problem is I think he's right."

Sara gently placed a hand on the other woman's back. "Then why not give him another chance?"

Laurie's head jolted up, the color returning to her face. "Another chance? Why the hell should I give him another chance?" She let loose with an unladylike snort, then covered her mouth. "I'm sorry, that was unprofessional of me. You won't hear that kind of outburst from me again."

"Stop apologizing! I want you to be yourself around me. If that includes the occasional rant at your ex-husband, I'll live with it."

"You really won't care if I gather up all the newspapers in town and build a bonfire on

Kenny's front lawn?" Laurie railed. "Or call him an ingrate who didn't know a good thing when he had it? Because nobody loved that man like I did, and that sure as hell includes Chrissy, who didn't love him at all."

"Chrissy Coleman?" Sara asked in surprise. "Quincy Coleman's daughter?"

"You've heard of her. She was Kenny's high-school girlfriend before she dumped him for Mike Donahue. Who, by the way, looks even better than he did in high school. I just ran into him downstairs."

Laurie's story wasn't making sense.

"You don't have a problem with Michael?" Sara asked.

"Of course not," Laurie said. "When we were teenagers, he was my hero."

The words were strikingly like the first ones Sara had ever spoken to Michael. "How so?"

"I was head over heels for Kenny. Kenny was crazy about Chrissy. And Chrissy, well, Chrissy had her sights set on Mike. She begged him to take her with him when he left Indigo Springs. That was fine by me, idiot that I was back then. It left me a clear path to Kenny."

"That's not the way I heard it," Sara said thoughtfully. "I heard Michael sweet-talked Chrissy into leaving."

"Yeah, well. That's the thing about small towns. You have to take what you hear with a whole shaker of salt and make your own mind up about people."

It wasn't until much later, when Sara ventured downstairs to close the windows that had been left open to air out the office, that Sara gave serious thought as to what her office manager had advised.

Laurie had told her to make up her own mind.

Sara yanked the first window closed. Isn't that what she had done when she followed her heart to Indigo Springs? Hadn't she vowed to quit doing what others expected of her and to be true to herself?

She positioned her fingers on the latch of the second window. Didn't being true to herself involve choosing her own friends, without regard for people who tried to convince her she didn't know her own mind?

Hadn't she made up her mind about Michael long before now?

She tugged on the window but nothing happened. She tried exerting more force, but the window still wouldn't budge. She moved back, arms crossed over her chest, wrestling with her problems.

Getting the window closed was minor. Getting

Michael back into her life, however briefly, was major.

An idea occurred to her. Before she could consider its wisdom, she located her cell phone and found the phone number she wanted.

"Michael," she said when she heard his voice. "It's Sara. Could you come by? It's going to be dark soon, and I can't close one of the windows you left open."

CHAPTER SEVEN

MICHAEL CLICKED OFF his cell phone, pocketed it and ran a hand over his lower face.

"Trouble?" Johnny asked.

Michael had stopped by Pollock Construction to return the sander he'd borrowed and caught Johnny closing up for the day. His friend seemed so eager to go home to his bride that Michael had tabled plans to invite him out for a burger and a beer.

"Nothing like that," he said, "but you got any spray lubricant I can borrow?"

"Sure. What for?"

"Uh, my, um, aunt. There's a window she can't get to shut."

"You're a terrible liar." Johnny went behind a counter, ducked down and handed him the bottle of lubricant. "Want to tell me who that really was?"

Michael figured there was no point in keeping up the fiction. "Sara Brenneman."

"And she wants you to shut her window?" Johnny's tone conveyed his skepticism.

"It's stuck."

Johnny laughed and slapped him on the back. "Sure it is."

The window *was* stuck, although it turned out Michael didn't need the spray lubricant. A little elbow grease worked just fine. He was fastening the latch and wondering why Sara hadn't asked one of her neighbors to wrestle the troublesome window closed when the office door swung open.

"That'll be the pizza," she said brightly, as though they'd agreed to make a night of it. "Half pepperoni and half mushrooms. I took a chance you'd like one or the other."

He stayed where he was while she dealt with the delivery man, deciding she looked more like a teenager than a lawyer in blue-jean shorts and a yellow T-shirt. The tangy scent of tomato sauce, cheese and pepperoni drifted toward him and his mouth watered, but he wouldn't swear the pizza was the source.

"We better get upstairs and eat this while it's hot," she announced when the delivery man was gone, her light-brown eyes wide and earnest.

"I don't remember us making plans to have dinner."

"We didn't," she said, "although now that you're here, you might as well eat."

She headed for the staircase, assuming he'd follow her. After a moment's hesitation in which he discovered his willpower was weak, he did. When he got to the second floor, she'd already set the pizza box on her kitchen table.

"Are you up for beer?" Without waiting for his answer, she yanked open the refrigerator door. "I'm not a big drinker, but beer always tastes good with pizza."

After setting two bottles of ale on the laminate countertop, she pulled a can opener out of a drawer and popped off the caps. "Paper plates and napkins are on the top shelf in that long, thin closet. We'll eat outside on the deck."

"I don't remember saying I was staying," he protested, although he couldn't imagine leaving now. This glimpse of how she operated when she had her mind set on something was too intriguing. It remained to be seen exactly what she planned to do next.

"Of course you're staying. I heard your stomach growl." She picked up the beer bottles. "You get the pizza, napkins and paper plates."

Surrendering to the inevitable, he did as she asked. The wooden deck, which was tucked into the sloped hillside, flowed from the house and afforded a great deal of privacy. He looked over the side, locating the posts dug into the ground, admiring the architect who'd made the most of the space allotted.

"I love it out here at twilight." She was already seated on one of the two wicker chairs positioned on either side of a small glass-top table. "My neighborhood in D.C. was never quiet, not even in the middle of the night. This is like my own little slice of heaven."

"Funny," he said. "Indigo Springs has always felt like hell to me."

"That's harsh."

"My car's in front of your house. The longer it stays, the more gossip there'll be."

She turned a clear-eyed look on him. "So what?"

"What are you doing, Sara? We agreed to keep things between us strictly business."

"I didn't agree to anything." Her chin had a stubborn tilt.

"You didn't *dis*agree. Not after you found out why people around here aren't happy to see me back."

"*Some* people," she corrected. "I've decided not to listen to what they say about you."

He closed his eyes and kneaded the bridge of his nose. She knew who he was and what he'd done, yet she still looked at him with tenderness. Something equally soft turned over inside him. The argument he'd been about to make about how a single good deed couldn't make up for his past leeched out of him.

Sara kept the conversation going until they'd had their fill of pizza, explaining the steps she was taking to build her business, asking why he'd gone into construction.

They cleared the plates when they were finished, bringing them into the house to dump them into the wastebasket.

"I should be going," he said. "I don't want people to talk any more than they're already going to."

"I already told you I don't care what people say."

"A friendship works two ways, Sara." They weren't separated by more than a foot in her small kitchen. "If we're going to be friends, you've got to let me have some say."

"Is that all you want from me?" she asked. "Friendship?"

"Yes," he said quickly.

"You're an awful liar," she said. It was the second time today he'd been told the same thing.

"How do you know I'm lying?"

She put her hands on his chest, which brought

her lower body into contact with his. His erection was straining against his jeans.

"That's how," she said.

She was tall enough that their mouths were just inches apart. He read the invitation in her eyes. To take her up on it, he only needed to lower his mouth.

"I'm still leaving town," he said. "Maybe as early as Saturday."

"Does anyone ever tell you to lighten up?"

The question was so unexpected he laughed. "No."

"Well, they should. Because you think way too much."

"Isn't thinking a good thing?"

"In your case, no. Don't you ever just do what you want and damn the consequences?"

That hadn't been the way he'd operated in a very long time. Experience had taught him to consider all possible outcomes before he acted, the way he should consider them now. His brain didn't seem to be cooperating though, not when he could smell the clean scent of her and feel her warm breath on his mouth.

"Aw, hell," he said an instant before he dipped his head and kissed her.

He'd been trying to block the taste of her from his mind since Monday night, when they'd kissed on the porch swing. He'd convinced himself kissing her couldn't possibly feel as good as he remembered.

He was right.

It was even better.

Her mouth was pliant beneath his, as though they'd kissed a hundred times instead of just a few. Their noses didn't bump, their teeth didn't grind and they seemed to know exactly what pleased the other.

He smoothed a hand down the length of her back, pressing her against him. She came willingly, making sexy little sounds back in her throat.

She was close, but he wanted her closer. His hand drifted even lower, over the curve of her bottom and down the bare skin of her thigh. He couldn't seem to stop touching her. His hand glided up and over her hip. Her T-shirt had ridden up, exposing the smooth skin of her waist. He stroked her, then his hand ventured higher, cupping her breast.

She pressed her breast into his palm, her warm tongue thrusting into his mouth. He heard his own harsh breathing. He was losing control fast, the way he had on the porch swing that night, the way he seemed to whenever she was in his arms.

The distinct sound of glass breaking pierced his consciousness.

He lifted his head, hoping one of them had bumped an end table or a curio cabinet and knocked a glass to the floor. He already knew he wouldn't find anything because the sound had come from downstairs.

"Did you hear that?" he asked, his voice uneven.

She stared up at him, her pupils wide, her mouth well-kissed, her long hair disheveled. "I don't care what it was."

He swallowed, wishing he could adopt the same cavalier attitude, but it was impossible, especially since he had a good guess what had happened. "It'll only take a few minutes to check out."

He heard frustration in her sigh before she unwound her arms from his neck. One of his hands was still in her hair, the other on the warm skin just below her breast. Abruptly he let her go. "It came from downstairs."

He preceded her down the steps, his gaze immediately zeroing in on the window that had been so hard to close. A hole pierced the center of the glass, radiating outward in a starburst pattern.

"Damn it," he exclaimed.

It took only seconds to find the rock, even though it was surprisingly small, only two or three inches in diameter. He held it out to Sara. "I told you my car shouldn't be parked in front of your place."

"You think someone broke my window because of you?" She sounded incredulous, unwilling to accept what he knew was true.

"It makes sense," he said, thinking of Quincy Coleman and Kenny Grieb. Either one could have sent a warning message.

"It makes *no* sense," she retorted. "That's not a rock. It's a pebble! If somebody wanted to send a message, they would have sent a louder one than a pebble makes."

Michael examined the rock, unwilling to call it a pebble or concede her point. He wasn't imagining things. There were people in town who hated him. "What other explanation could there be?"

A pounding on the front door stopped her from answering.

She raised her eyebrows. "I'd say we're about to find out."

She opened the door to reveal a middle-aged woman and a tall, lanky boy of about thirteen or fourteen. The woman's lips were thinned and the boy looked miserable. The woman nudged the boy. "Go ahead."

"I'm sorry." The boy stared down at his feet.

"Tell her what you're sorry for," the woman prompted. "And look her in the eye."

The boy's head rose, but his gaze still didn't quite meet Sara's. "I didn't mean to break your window. I was trying to hit the street sign."

The woman held up a slingshot. "We own the sporting goods store down the street. Donny told me that Ben took this from inventory."

"Miserable little tattletale," Ben said under his breath.

"Don't talk about your brother that way," the woman scolded. "I'm Edna Stanton, by the way. We live above our store, too. I've been meaning to welcome you to town, but not this way."

Sara smiled. "I'm Sara Brenneman and this is Michael Donahue."

Michael tensed, waiting for the woman to recognize his name, but she greeted them both cordially. Then she nudged the boy again.

"I've got some money saved up," Ben said. "I'll pay for the damage."

"Darned right you will," his mother said.

After they were gone, Sara leaned back against the closed door and simply looked at him. "Well?"

"I don't blame Ben for being mad at his little brother," he said. "His mom was scary."

"I was talking about the broken window and

you know it," she said. "It didn't have anything
to do with you."

"It could have." He hadn't been careful
enough after the anonymous call and the
slashed tires. It hadn't occurred to him that the
women around him might be targets. "I need to
check out my aunt's house."

She pressed her lips together, her thoughts a
mystery.

"Are you sure?"

He could have told her he wasn't sure of
anything when he was around her, but then
she'd touch him or kiss him and his brain would
shut off again. "I'm sure."

This time he thought he pulled off the lie, but
that fact didn't bring him satisfaction.

SARA KEPT her face expressionless, an achieve-
ment she was perfecting through practice.

She'd managed not to expose her feelings
last night after a rock—no, a pebble—had
stopped Michael from finishing what she'd
started. Neither had she reacted this morning
when Michael told her he wasn't coming to the
appointment at the bank.

Her poker face was firmly fixed now as
though Sara wasn't dismayed to learn that the
stout, balding branch manager was an unfortu-
nate anomaly.

Unlike the majority of town residents, he was a transplant.

"Moved here from Harrisburg a year ago in February," Art Price said in response to Sara's question. "The job opportunity was too good to pass up."

"So you don't know Mrs. Feldman?" Sara gestured to the woman occupying one of the straight-backed chairs in Art's office. She made a mental note never to buy uncomfortable office furniture.

Felicia Feldman was twisting her hands in her habitual nervous gesture. Sara captured one of them for a reassuring squeeze, although she couldn't predict how the meeting would turn out.

What mattered at the moment was that they appear confident, just as what mattered last night was that Michael never know how much his latest rejection stung.

She was determined not to give him a chance to turn her down again. She'd decided his baggage was far too heavy for her to carry.

"I know Mrs. Feldman now." Price picked up a stack of papers and riffled through them, bringing Sara's attention full-circle. "I'm curious as to why you took out this loan, Mrs. Feldman. The monthly payments seem high for someone at your income level."

"My husband took out the loan without telling me." Mrs. Feldman stared down at her hands. "I'm ashamed to say I signed the papers without reading them."

"Never a good idea." Price pushed his wire-rimmed glasses up his nose. "You should have contacted us as soon as you knew you'd have a problem making the payments."

"She did," Sara said, then explained the bills had been sent to a post-office box Mrs. Feldman didn't know about until after her husband's death. "But you raised a good point. Why did your bank give the Feldmans a loan when it was clear they'd have trouble making the payments?"

"I can't enlighten you on decisions that were made before I started working here," Price said. "It's water under the bridge anyway. All I can do is speak to the current situation."

"We'd like you to refinance the loan, with the missed payments being folded into the new loan," Sara stated. "If you need to extend the terms of the new loan so the payments are manageable, that's fine."

Price peered at her over the top of his glasses. "Would you, now?"

"Yes," Sara said, undeterred. "We'd also like you to reduce the closing costs and cut the interest rate as a courtesy to Mrs. Feldman since she's been banking here for years."

"You're asking for an awful lot considering I haven't agreed to refinance," Price said. "You must realize this isn't standard procedure."

"Neither is letting longtime customers put up their home for collateral on a loan they can barely afford, yet that's exactly what happened."

"Mr. Feldman must have been advised of the disadvantages."

"We don't know that for sure, do we?" Sara smiled to soften the sting in her words. "So I'd think a bank as reputable as yours would be eager to keep a customer like Mrs. Feldman happy."

"Touché, Ms. Brenneman." Art Price's eyes twinkled with admiration. "I'd like to see what you can do in a courtroom some day, as long as I'm not on the opposing side."

"Right now, Mr. Price, I'd very much like to get you on our side."

He chuckled, although she meant every word. Until she'd picked up Mrs. Feldman this morning, Sara had viewed the situation from a purely practical standpoint. If the bank foreclosed, Mrs. Feldman would be dealt a severe financial hit from which she might never recover.

The silent tears that had clouded Mrs. Feldman's eyes during the drive to the bank had brought home to Sara that a lot more than money was at stake. Losing her house would mean losing her sanctuary, the only place she'd ever felt she belonged.

"I can't give you an answer immediately," Price said. "I need to run this up the ladder, then get my loan officer to work out the details of a new loan."

"When will we know your decision?" Sara asked.

"Possibly the end of business today, more likely some time on Monday." He tapped the business card she'd given him. "I'll give you a call as soon as I know."

The sun was shining when they exited the bank, which Sara thought was appropriate. If she'd read the signals correctly, it looked as though Mrs. Feldman would keep her house.

"I thought it went okay," Mrs. Feldman said, echoing her thoughts. She cast an anxious glance at Sara. "How did you think it went?"

"You never can tell about these things, so let's just say I'm cautiously optimistic," Sara said carefully, then pressed the crosswalk button at the intersection containing one of the town's two red lights. "I'll walk you to your car."

Mrs. Feldman had parked across the street in front of Jimmy's Diner. As they waited for the light to turn green, Quincy Coleman exited the restaurant. He turned as though intending to head south on the sidewalk, then looked directly at them. After a loaded pause, he changed directions, stopping on the opposite curb.

"What do you think of Quincy Coleman?" Sara asked under her breath.

"I don't like him." Mrs. Feldman stated her opinion with uncharacteristic force. "Never have. He's probably the one who gave Murray the loan. He always did have too much influence over him."

"Coleman and Murray were friends?"

"Close friends. Why do you think Murray disliked Michael so much?"

The light changed to green, temporarily preventing them from continuing the discussion as they stepped into the street. Coleman walked toward them, dressed as usual in business attire, this time a tan sports coat and navy slacks.

"Good morning, Felicia, Ms. Brenneman." He greeted them in the crosswalk, his smiled forced. The false friendliness made Sara suspicious, as though he were up to something, a notion that strengthened when he disappeared inside the bank.

"I don't trust that man," Sara remarked when

they reached the opposite side of the street. "What did you mean by Coleman having influence over Murray?"

"He's the one who convinced Murray to kick Michael out of the house." Mrs. Feldman wouldn't meet Sara's eyes as they walked the few steps to her car. "Michael's never forgiven me for allowing that to happen."

"Have you talked to him about it?"

"What would I say?" she asked miserably, the bright sun illuminating the regret on her face. "That I was a rotten aunt?"

"You could say you were sorry."

"It's too late for that. It wouldn't change the past."

"It's never too late," Sara said, although when the phone call from the bank came through at just before five o'clock she doubted her own words.

Once his aunt's problem was solved and Michael left town, Mrs. Feldman would lose her chance to make peace with him. And Sara would lose Michael.

There she went again, she chided herself. She couldn't lose a man she'd never had in the first place.

She ignored the regret that swept through her and clicked on the phone, adopting her most professional voice. "Sara Brenneman."

"Ms. Brenneman. It's Mr. Price. I have bad news. That new loan we talked about didn't go through."

Sara would have been surprised had the bank refinanced under the terms she had requested. In her experience, though, it was always best to ask for too much than settle for too little.

"Then I'll come in first thing Monday and see if we can come up with alternate terms agreeable to both of us," she said.

"I'm afraid you don't understand." His voice was firm and businesslike, the levity of this morning gone. "We can't refinance her loan at all."

"What! Why?" she asked, even as she flashed to Quincy Coleman going into the bank that morning after they'd left.

"We ran her credit report and it's not a good risk for us."

"But her late husband was responsible for ruining her credit," Sara said. "Mrs. Feldman had nothing to do with it."

"The credit report reflects equally on both of them, Ms. Brenneman," he said in a scholarly tone. "You know that."

Sara also knew Price had been perfectly amenable to refinancing this morning. "Can you at least extend the deadline?"

She heard the sound of the branch manager's throat clearing. "I'm sorry, but no. Please tell Mrs. Feldman if she doesn't pay the amount, she's in default, and we'll be forced to initiate foreclosure proceedings. I recommend putting the house up for sale."

Every instinct Sara possessed screamed that Quincy Coleman was behind the reversal, but she'd been a lawyer long enough to refrain from leveling an accusation without proof. If she was wrong—and, possibly, even if she wasn't—she risked making an enemy.

She had no choice but to accept Mr. Price's decision.

For now.

Once she turned the matter over in her head, she'd decide what she could do about it.

CHAPTER EIGHT

SARA HAD NEVER BEEN one to prolong the agony.

She thought it better to tear the Band-Aid from a wound in one quick motion than to peel it off gradually. If the water in a pool was too cold, she'd rather dive in and absorb the shock all at once than descend a ladder and wade into the deep end.

But by Saturday morning, she still hadn't relayed the bank's bad news to Felicia Feldman.

It was easy to justify the delay as a consequence of her busy life.

After getting the call from Art Price, she'd accepted a last-minute invitation to grab some dinner with the receptionist who worked next door. This morning she'd been recruited to help the Friends of the Indigo Springs Library with their semi-annual used-book sale.

But the real reason Sara hadn't yet accepted failure was that all indications had pointed to success.

It was as though she was waiting for Quincy Coleman to come into the library and apologize for sabotaging Sara's efforts. While he was at it, he might even offer to reverse the damage.

Like that was going to happen.

Sara straightened the paperbacks in the rapidly dwindling romance section, then reached into the cardboard box under the table to add more books.

"How are you doing?" Marie Dombrowski bustled over to her table, her smile as friendly as it had been at the wedding where they'd met.

Sara smiled. "Business is brisk. I can hardly keep the table stocked."

"I'm so glad we have a volunteer who's a romance reader." Marie patted her hand. "But then I'm just glad to have another volunteer. We're having such a great turnout we need all the bodies we can get."

A steady stream of people pored over books, videos and old magazines laid out by genre on tables in a meeting room barely big enough to hold the sale.

The library itself was rich in charm but lacking in space. Housed in a small brick building that sat atop a grassy knoll, it had been built at the turn of the twentieth century.

"Keep them moving," Marie said. "The more

money we take in, the closer we get to paying for an addition."

"Aye, aye, captain." Sara saluted, earning her a laugh.

Time passed swiftly. Sara had agreed to help because she loved books, but she was meeting so many people it was turning into a fabulous networking opportunity. Half of them asked for her business card, the other half for recommendations.

"Depends on whether you want to laugh or cry," Sara told a young woman with curly white-blond hair and freckles. She seemed familiar but Sara couldn't place her.

"Laugh," the young woman said instantly.

"Try Crusie or Philips, unless you're into vampires or werewolves. Then you might want to give Maryjanice Davidson a shot."

"Vampires are way hotter than werewolves. I personally can't get excited by a hero with back hair." The romance reader spoke enthusiastically, then giggled. "I'm Dee Dee Powlaski. I know I sound like a nut, but I'm actually respectable. I even work at a bank."

"That's where I've seen you before. You're a teller at Indigo Springs Bank, aren't you?"

"Yes," Dee Dee said, smiling.

Sara introduced herself, taking another opportunity to hand out a business card. "I was in your bank yesterday."

Dee Dee nodded. "I know. I saw you with Mr. Price."

Sara's heartbeat quickened. Here, when she least expected it, was her chance to get some insider information about what had gone wrong with Mrs. Feldman's refinancing request. She made her tone casual. "Were you working at the bank when Quincy Coleman was president?"

"Yes, I was. In fact, he hired me." Dee Dee tucked some strands of blond hair behind her ear. "Do you know Mr. Coleman?"

"Not well."

"Me neither," Dee Dee said. "He retired after I'd been at the bank a few months."

"How long ago was that?"

Dee Dee paused to think. "Let's see. I started working there a year ago in March. So it must have been last May."

Sara remembered Mr. Price confiding that he'd been employed at the bank for about a year and immediately connected the dots. "So Mr. Coleman hired Mr. Price."

"That's right. It was kind of surprising with Mr. Price being from out of town, but Mr. Coleman took a liking to him right away. Mr. Coleman still comes in three or four times a week to visit. He was at the bank only yesterday."

"He wasn't there to do his banking?"

"Oh, no. He went right to Mr. Price's office and closed the door." Dee Dee lowered her voice, as though confiding a secret. "I think he likes to keep up on what's happening. Why are you asking all these questions anyway?"

To confirm my suspicions, Sara thought.

"No particular reason," Sara said. "I'm just trying to get to know the people in town."

"Then maybe you'll want to join my book club," Dee Dee said. "There are seven of us. We all like different kinds of books so it's a great way to explore new authors."

"I'd like that," Sara said, her mind still on Quincy Coleman.

By the time the book sale ended, she still couldn't figure out how to use what she'd learned about the man to her advantage.

After stopping by her office to check out the painted walls, which were drying nicely, she figured it was time to brief Michael's aunt on the unhappy status of her case.

Except it wasn't Mrs. Feldman she encountered when she got to the house on Oak Street. Michael looked up from where he was hammering a new board into place on the porch steps, his face damp with sweat. His body tensed as though bracing himself for her to do something as stupid as she'd done the other night when she'd walked into his arms.

Well, that was too bad.

She had business with his aunt and she wasn't about to turn tail just because she made him uncomfortable.

She wouldn't walk into his arms, either. If there was a next move, which she seriously doubted at this point, it would have to come from him.

"I had a look at the office." She willed herself to keep the conversation impersonal, business-woman to businessman. "You did a great job."

"Thank you," he said. That was it, just thank you.

His grayish-blue eyes seemed to bore into her, asking questions she didn't dare answer.

"I'm not here to see you," she blurted.

"I didn't think you were."

"Good. I'm glad that's settled." She strove to hide her bubbling anger, upset with herself for letting it form.

"My aunt won't be back until tomorrow morning. She's staying with a friend who had cataract surgery." He wiped his brow with the back of one sleeve. "Is this about her loan?"

Since technically Michael was the one who'd

hired her, she might as well tell him. "Yes. The bank called to say they won't refinance."

He put down his hammer and gave her his full attention, his brow knitted.

"The branch manager recommended she try to sell the house before they foreclose, but I'd like to avoid that." She outlined the strategy she'd worked out. "I'll continue to contact other lenders to see if they're more open to refinancing, but it's a tough road because of her poor credit."

"Hold on." He held up a hand. "I thought her best chance to refinance was at the bank where people know her. She said you were optimistic things would work out."

"I was," she said.

"Then what happened?"

An image formed of Quincy Coleman entering the bank minutes after they'd exited. "I can't say for sure."

"But you suspect something." He kept his sharp gaze on her, waiting for her to continue.

"You're right, I do," she finally said. It was pointless to keep the information from him when he might help her figure out how to act on her suspicions. "Quincy Coleman visited the bank yesterday."

He stiffened. "And?"

"And today I found out he was behind closed

doors with the branch manager, who, by the way, he hired."

"You think Coleman convinced the branch manager not to refinance my aunt's loan?" Michael asked, arriving at the same conclusion she had. His barely leashed anger made her question whether she should have told him, but it was too late to backtrack.

"Yeah, I do."

"Son of a bitch," he bit out, letting the anger flow. "His problem is with me, not my aunt."

"It's just a theory, Michael." She personally believed the assumption had teeth but felt compelled to offer another explanation. "It's possible Mr. Coleman's visit was coincidental. The bank could have turned down our request because your aunt's late husband ruined her credit."

"That's not the reason," he said, through clenched teeth.

"The reason doesn't matter." She voiced the conclusion she'd reluctantly reached a few hours ago. "The bank turned us down and we can't do anything about it."

"I don't agree."

He stood up, dusting off his jeans. Without another word, he disappeared into the house and reappeared a moment later with car keys. His face was set, his expression determined.

"What are you going to do?" she asked

"What I should have done a long time ago," he said. "It's time Quincy Coleman and I had this out."

FOR THE second time in his life, Michael waited on the doorstep of the large, elegant Victorian house where Quincy Coleman lived alone.

The first time, Michael had been a nervous seventeen-year-old kid, Mr. Coleman's wife hadn't yet left him and Chrissy had been a pretty girl Michael wanted to know better.

Mr. Coleman had answered the door, dressed in a suit as though he'd just come from work. Michael remembered stammering when he introduced himself and not mustering enough poise to offer the older man his hand.

Coleman wouldn't have taken it anyway.

"You've got a lot of nerve coming around my daughter," Coleman had said through clenched teeth. "You don't belong here. Just leave and don't come back."

Before Michael could say a word, Coleman had slammed the door in his face.

The chilly reception hadn't come entirely as a surprise. Chrissy had warned him her father was a snob who vehemently opposed her dating a high-school kid straight out of juvenile detention.

Not getting a chance to stick up for himself and explain his determination to turn his life around had rankled, making Michael more resolute than ever to pursue the man's daughter.

He used to wait near the big oak tree in the backyard for Chrissy to sneak out of the house. She'd been more sexually experienced than Michael so he never felt like he was taking advantage of her. One time they'd done it under the tree with the full moon shining down on them.

A part of him had hoped Coleman would look out his bedroom window that night and catch them in the act.

Michael had grown up in the last nine years, but enough of that teenage defiance remained that he stood straight and proud on the porch steps he'd been told never again to cross.

He rang the doorbell once more, pressing for a full ten seconds. No answer. Michael still wasn't prepared to concede that Coleman wasn't home.

Determination fueling his steps, he left the porch and circled the house. He wasn't a teenager anymore. He'd learned you couldn't solve a problem by skulking in the shadows. The only way to tackle one was head-on.

The spacious backyard extended into a thicket of woods. It was as deserted as the front, but bits of grass stuck to the bottoms of Michael's shoes and the lawn had that just-mowed smell. A sidewalk led from the rear porch to a detached garage a good distance from the main house.

Michael had a side view of the garage but could see Coleman's silver Cadillac parked in the driveway. He approached the free-standing building, finding the tilt-up door standing wide-open.

The interior of the garage was fastidiously kept, with tools hanging from pegboard and old kitchen cabinets lining a side wall. An off-road motorcycle, a lawn mower and a mountain bike occupied one half of the parking space. On the empty half, Coleman, dressed in an old pair of khakis and a T-shirt, dumped clippings from his mower bag into a tall yard-waste bag.

Coleman looked up, some of the clippings falling on the floor. His expression instantly hardened. "You've got a hell of a lot of nerve coming here."

The words were almost identical to the ones Coleman had hurled at Michael all those years ago, but they were slurred. Michael's gaze swept the garage, picking out empty beer cans on the counter before refastening on the enraged Coleman.

Michael unclenched the fists at his side and tried to let go of the long-ago resentment this visit to Coleman's house had stirred. Anger wouldn't get him anywhere. "I'm here to make peace between us."

Coleman's face turned red and the veins in his temples bulged. "I should spit in your face."

Michael flinched. The older man's all-consuming hatred was as fresh and raw as it had been eight years ago when Michael had accompanied Chrissy's body back to Indigo Springs. He'd barely choked out how sorry he was before Coleman lit into him, the same way he was now.

When he was nineteen, Michael didn't have the strength to go against Coleman's wishes. Unwilling to risk another ugly scene, he'd stayed away from Chrissy's funeral.

Now the time for retreat was over, even though the remorse and regret had never left him.

"Hear me out before you do anything," Michael said. "I know I can't make up for what you lost, but—"

"You're damn right you can't," Coleman bit out, taking a step closer. His breath reeked of beer.

Michael continued, determined to say what he'd come to say. "I was sorry then, and I'm sorry now. I hope we can at least find a way to be civil to each other."

"Civil?" Coleman spewed out the word. "You son of a bitch. You took my daughter from me. You ruined my marriage. And now you come here and dare talk to me about being civil?"

"I understand you hate me," Michael began.

"*Hate* doesn't begin to cover it."

"I even understand why you slashed my tires."

"You're lucky I didn't slash your throat." Coleman's face was turning redder by the second.

"Just leave my aunt out of this. She has nothing to do with any of it."

"You're living in her house. That makes her part of it."

"I'm only living there until—"

"You shouldn't be here. In this town. On my property."

"But I—"

"Get out!" Coleman yelled. "Get out before I call the police!"

Michael hesitated, torn between getting far away from Coleman and staying to explain he'd leave town if Aunt Felicia got to keep her house.

"Get out!" Coleman yelled again, his voice booming.

Michael backed away, realizing he couldn't

reason with a drunk man. Coleman didn't have the capacity to understand his interference at the bank had prolonged Michael's stay in town instead of shortening it.

"Don't come here again!" Coleman shouted.

Michael kept walking, helpless to stop the on-slaught of angry words or to prevent Coleman's neighbors from hearing them.

It was a Saturday afternoon like any other with a fair number of people outside enjoying the warm, summer day.

A couple of kids on the sidewalk straddled their bikes, leveling twin stares. A woman kneeling in front of a flower bed at the house across the street looked up from her gardening. A man next door stood by a lawn mower, his gaze riveted. Michael recognized him. It was Kenny Grieb, whose parents were long-time neighbors of the Colemans.

"You hear me, Donahue!" Coleman shouted. "Next time I'll have you arrested!"

Shame rose up in Michael like the Lehigh River water during a storm, although he'd done nothing wrong.

Not this time.

He felt the cold stares of Kenny Grieb and Coleman's other neighbors and turned deliber-ately away from them only to see Sara rushing toward him. Her car was parked directly behind his.

The tide of humiliation almost knocked him over. Having Sara there, witnessing the ugly scene, made it so much worse.

"You shouldn't have followed me." His raw emotions made his voice hoarse.

"Of course I should have. You hired me to be your aunt's lawyer, remember?"

"That's right!" Coleman was standing at the foot of the driveway, still shouting. "Get out!"

Michael continued to his car, Sara keeping pace with him. "Let's go have a cup of coffee and talk about this."

He opened the door to his car and slipped inside before he looked up at her. He saw the last thing he wanted from her—pity.

"There's nothing to talk about," he said. "Coleman didn't admit to anything."

"We could still have that coffee," she offered.

"No thanks." He pulled the car door shut.

She looked as if he'd slapped her, striking his conscience a blow, but any conversation they had would only result in Sara offering to talk to Coleman. That might be the wisest course of action, but this wasn't Sara's problem to solve. It was his.

Whenever Coleman sobered up, Michael planned to make another stab at reasoning with him.

For his aunt's sake.

And maybe for his own, too.

"TELL ME everything about you and Michael Donahue, no matter how small the detail," Penelope demanded of Sara on Saturday night, her eyes shining with anticipation.

After Penelope had offered an unnecessary apology for not getting together sooner, they'd grabbed the last table at the Blue Haven Pub, a neighborhood hangout almost free of tourists. Conversation flowed around them, competing with the soft rock music coming from the juke-box and the sound from two small televisions above the bar showing a Phillies game. Penelope's husband had excused himself to get them drinks.

"There's nothing to tell," Sara said with little hope Penelope would drop the subject. Her old high-school friend had turned into a match-maker the instant she'd donned a bridal veil.

Penelope did an exaggerated eye roll. "Oh, come on! Johnny said you and Michael were an item. Besides, I saw you at the wedding. Do you really expect me to believe you're not interested?"

"I make it a policy not to be interested in men who aren't interested in me," Sara said.

Penelope frowned. "What does that mean? And talk fast before Michael gets here."

"Michael's coming here?"

"Should be here any minute." The huge smile that suddenly wreathed Penelope's face telegraphed to Sara that Johnny was approaching the table from behind Sara. Penelope didn't smile like that at anyone else. "Isn't that right, Johnny?"

Johnny set three long-necked bottles of beer on the table before kissing his wife enthusiastically on the lips as though they'd been apart for five days instead of five minutes. "Isn't what right, Pen?"

Penelope sighed with contentment before replying. "I was just telling Sara that Michael's joining us."

Johnny grimaced. "Not anymore. He canceled."

"Why would he cancel?" Penelope cried as though she was the injured party. "You told him it was going to be the four of us, right?"

"He didn't say." Johnny avoided the question, but the answer was obvious. Michael wasn't coming because he knew Sara would be there.

"Okay." Penelope was already canvassing the bar with her eyes. "Then let's see who else we can match Sara up with."

"Penelope, stop!" Sara said. "I didn't move to Indigo Springs to find a man. I'm here to start a law practice."

"Who says you can't do both?" Penelope asked tartly, her gaze still sweeping the room. The good-looking man with the healthy tan who'd been best man at Johnny's wedding walked into the pub. "There's Chase, but we all know he's not available."

"I'm still asking him to join us," Johnny said with a laugh, motioning the man to their table. Sara remembered somebody saying he was some sort of park ranger. He looked the part, tall and rangy with the appearance of a man who spent a lot of time outdoors.

Chase met Sara's eyes and said all the right things when Johnny performed the introductions, but something was obviously troubling him.

"Have any of you seen Mandy?" he asked without sitting down, his eyes making the same scan of the bar as Penelope's had. "She left her son with my dad…"

His voice cut off, and Sara followed his line of vision. The woman he was living with, the one who'd yelled at Sara during the job interview, was emerging from the restroom. The short skirt she wore with a sleeveless black top was an attention-getter, but not as much as the bottle of beer she held.

"Excuse me," Chase said, then moved quickly through the maze of tables to intercept her.

"Isn't she pregnant?" Sara asked.

"I think Chase is about to point that out to her," Penelope said as they watched him lower his head to Mandy's, his body language telegraphing his disapproval. "But I've heard them have this out before. Mandy says the occasional beer doesn't hurt anything."

"And she has another child?" Sara asked.

"A little boy," Johnny said. "About a year old."

Mandy threw up the hand not holding the beer, headed straight for the bar and set down the bottle so hard liquid sloshed out of it. Then she stalked out of the bar. After a moment, Chase followed her.

"That little scene should put my wife off romance. At least for tonight." Johnny put an arm around Penelope, running his hand up and down her bare arm. "She's a shameless matchmaker."

"Me?" Penelope protested. "It was your idea to get Sara together with Michael. You said maybe some of her love for Indigo Springs would rub off on him."

"I don't understand," Sara said, focusing on Johnny.

"Michael got the official word today that he was approved for another assignment, this time in Ghana," Johnny said. "He has ten days to decide whether to accept it."

Sara tried not to show the prospect of Michael taking off for a west African country halfway around the world bothered her. "So?"

"So most people have had enough of the Peace Corps after two years," Johnny said. "Michael's been a volunteer for six."

"Then he must like it."

"He won't admit it, but he's burned out. It's time for him to get on with his life." Johnny took a pull from his beer and put the bottle down on the table with an audible thunk. "It's time for him to come home."

"He doesn't think of Indigo Springs as home." Against her good judgment, Sara let herself get pulled into the conversation. "He told me he'd never live here again."

"Because of Quincy Coleman." Johnny sounded disgusted. "That man should just leave Michael be."

"Then you heard what happened this afternoon?" Sara asked.

"Who didn't?" Johnny said. "Kenny Grieb was there, and he's the biggest gossip in town."

"I was also there," Sara said. "If someone yelled at me the way Coleman was yelling at Michael, I'd have a sour feeling about the town, too."

Johnny took a drink from his beer while he considered her statement, then slanted her a significant look. "Maybe you can convince Michael it's not so bad here."

She raised her eyebrows. "Me? Why me?"

"Michael likes you."

"If Michael liked me so much," Sara retorted, "he wouldn't avoid me."

"Not true," Johnny said. "He's staying away so he won't cause you any trouble."

"I'll tell you what I told him. I don't let anyone dictate who my friends are."

Johnny's face creased into a smile. "Then the four of us can have dinner together tomorrow night. I'll make sure Michael shows."

"I'll make a reservation," Penelope offered.

"Make it a reservation for three, because I'm not coming," Sara said firmly.

"Why not?" Johnny seemed genuinely confused. "You just said you don't care if people talk."

"I don't," Sara replied. "I also don't care to be set up with a man who doesn't want to be set up."

"But—" Johnny began.

"Give it a rest, Johnny," Sara interrupted. "I won't change my mind."

If Michael wanted to have dinner with her, he could ask her himself. Even then, she should tell him no.

The chances of either of those things happening was exactly nil.

CHAPTER NINE

KENNY WAS TRYING to drive her insane.

Laurie couldn't come up with any other explanation. Why else would he place that ridiculous ad in the *Indigo Springs Gazette* and then virtually ignore her?

After making the asinine suggestion that she call him to arrange to get together—yeah, right!—she hadn't heard one word from him.

She almost understood the silence on Friday. He was waiting her out, trying to see if she'd capitulate and call him.

But how to explain his standoffishness today? Had he lied about his willingness to give up alcohol? Was that it? Had he gone off somewhere and gotten so stinking drunk he'd forgotten his quest to win her back?

No sooner had she arrived at the theory than she was driving by the Blue Haven Pub, the place where Kenny had once spent most of his nonworking hours.

She happened to know it was still his favorite hangout because the butcher at the corner market revealed as much when she casually brought up the subject.

She parked her car at a curb two blocks down from the Blue Haven, hearing the rumbling of thunder in the distance when she got out of the car. The sky was darker than it should have been given that it wasn't yet sunset, and the air was heavy with the threat of rain.

She ought to get back in her car and drive home but she was already here. She walked casually toward the pub, encouraged that someone had left the door ajar.

It wouldn't hurt to peek inside.

She scanned the bar for Kenny, but her eyes fell on the reddish brown of her employer's hair. Sara sat at a table with Penelope and Johnny Pollock, the town newlyweds.

Laurie jumped back out of view, although she wasn't sure why. Sara wouldn't guess she was at the Blue Haven searching for Kenny. Nobody would.

"Hey, Laurie. You looking for Kenny?" The man seated at the bar stool nearest the door called. It was Mr. Gilroy, who lived three doors down from her mother. His wife had paid a visit yesterday toting her copy of the *Indigo Springs*

Gazette in case Laurie wanted an extra copy of the ad. She hadn't, but Mrs. Gilroy had left the newspaper behind anyway. "'Cause Kenny hasn't been by in maybe a week," Mr. Gilroy continued.

"Not looking for anyone," Laurie insisted. "Just passing by."

She waved to underscore her declaration, then hightailed it back to the car.

Just because Kenny wasn't at the Blue Haven didn't mean he wasn't drinking, but Laurie wasn't up to checking out all the bars in town after that close call. Besides, the weather was worsening by the second. The wind was gusting so hard she could hear it whistling, and the sky had darkened even more.

She guessed it was possible that Kenny wasn't out on the town but holed up in the little house on Harrison Street they used to share.

She was barely aware she'd decided to check out her theory when she found herself driving slowly down the block that had once held such charm for her.

It still did.

The tall, shady oak trees. The small, tidy houses. The wide, quiet street.

On the left the brick house she'd so loved was approaching, its front yard contained by a wood fence that a medium-sized white dog was hurdling.

Could that be Valentine, the shaggy-haired puppy she'd bought for Kenny their first Valentine's Day together?

Yes. It had to be. She recognized the black patch of fur on the dog's head, the tongue hanging from the side of her mouth that meant she was happy.

She was also on a suicide mission.

The dog dashed into the road, right into the path of her car. Laurie slammed on her brakes, her tires screeching on the pavement, narrowly avoiding her precious pet.

Her hands shook and her heart pounded as she pulled the car over to the curb. Keeping Val in her sights, she got out of the car on shaky legs.

The dog was already halfway down the block, joy in her prancing gait.

"Val!" she yelled above the whoosh of the wind. A paper fast-food bag blew into the street, tumbling end over end. "Valentine!"

The dog stopped, turned, one ear cocked.

"Come here, girl!" she yelled again.

Val took off for her at a gallop. Laurie crouched down and the dog launched herself into Laurie's arms, nearly knocking her over.

She laughed and felt tears dripping down her face. Or were those raindrops?

"I've missed you, too, girl," she said as she hugged the dog. "How could Kenny let you jump the fence like that?"

The answer came to her as clearly as the black patch on her beloved dog's head. He wouldn't. Kenny loved Val too much to leave the dog unattended in the yard if he knew she wasn't safe.

"What am I gonna do with you?" she asked the dog even though she already knew the answer.

She hurried across the street, Valentine in her arms, barely making it to the porch before the sky opened up, delivering sheets of rain.

"Don't think for one minute I'm here because of you," she said after Kenny opened the door and before he could get a word in. "I almost hit Valentine when she dashed in front of my car, and I wanted to let you know she can jump the fence."

She set Valentine down and the dog barked as though seconding her story.

"Valentine jumped the fence?" The cocky look that had been on Kenny's face when he greeted her disappeared, replaced by shock. He wasn't drunk. He wasn't with another woman. He was a man concerned about his dog.

Valentine took off, and Kenny followed her,

catching up to the dog in the family room. Laurie trailed him, anxious to assure herself he'd handle the problem and make sure Valentine never ran into the path of an oncoming car again.

Kenny knelt down, running his hands over the dog's fur and examining her for injuries.

"Val's fine," Laurie said. "But you have to watch her more carefully to make sure she doesn't get away from you again."

He turned, his eyes meeting hers, his expression intense. She mentally replayed what she'd just told him. He stood up, his eyes fastened on hers as he advanced. She told herself to retreat but her feet didn't move.

"That's what I've been trying to tell you, Laurie," he said. "I let you go once, but this time I'm gonna hold on."

He was within a foot of her when the lights went out, plunging the house into darkness. She felt familiar arms reach for her and tried to steel herself against his touch. She reminded herself he'd started a drunken fight with Mike Donahue over Chrissy Coleman a mere week ago.

But she smelled his clean, male scent instead of alcohol, and she didn't want to think about the origin of the grudge he still held against Michael.

Then he was kissing her exactly the way she liked to be kissed, and she was kissing him back, telling herself he was no longer hung up on Chrissy Coleman because she desperately wanted it to be true.

The darkness enveloping them made everything seem surreal. Like a dream. As she lost herself in sensation, though, she felt as if she'd finally awakened from her seven-year nightmare.

MICHAEL'S second visit to Quincy Coleman's house in less than twenty-four hours started the same way as the first, with no one answering the front door.

He took an identical path to the back of the house, acknowledging the differences. The ground was wet from last night's storm, the hour early enough that most of the neighbors were at Sunday services instead of in their yards and his eyes felt gritty from lack of sleep.

His determination to confront Coleman hadn't wavered, but his mission was more clear. He'd spent the previous evening alone in Aunt Felicia's house, lighting candles when the power went out, trying to read when the electricity came back on. But his mind had been on his problem rather than the latest edition of *Baseball Digest*.

If he'd figured out anything during his nearly sleepless night, it was that Coleman didn't understand the situation. Michael needed only a few minutes to explain that Coleman's sabotage of his aunt's loan had backfired.

If Coleman let the loan go through, Michael would leave town.

As simple as that.

Hell, he'd even promise never to come back if that made any difference.

He wondered if it would make any difference to Sara.

Thrusting her out of his mind, where he couldn't afford to let her be, he continued to the back of the house. The soles of his shoes made squishing noises in the wet grass.

He climbed the three wet wooden steps that led to the back porch, and stopped, surprised to see the back door ajar. A puddle of water had collected inside the house. The rain had stopped at around ten the night before, with the power being restored an hour or so later. Could Coleman's door have been open since then?

Michael pushed the door, the hinges squeaking as it slowly opened wide. A mourning dove cooed nearby, but inside the house the silence seemed deathly.

"Mr. Coleman?" Michael raised his voice. "Mr. Coleman, are you home?"

No answer.

His narrow view of the kitchen included a corner of the table and a portion of the counter. A bottle was overturned, amber liquid spilling from it.

Was that whiskey?

He inhaled and caught the scent of alcohol, looked down and spotted broken glass on the floor.

He stepped across the threshold, into the house. He briefly considered that Coleman could rightfully shoot him dead for trespassing, but he didn't turn back.

Something wasn't right here.

The smell of alcohol got stronger as he walked deeper into the kitchen. A shattered glass and broken plate were on the floor, along with what looked like the remnants of a hamburger and potato chips. Chairs had been upended and a thin streak of blood stained one wall.

"Mr. Coleman?" Michael called again.

Again, no answer.

Michael circled the counter, expecting to see the older man lying motionless on the floor, but nothing was there except another broken bottle and one more smashed plate.

"Mr. Coleman!" Michael moved swiftly through the house, steeling himself to find an injured—or worse—Quincy Coleman around every corner.

However, the downstairs was deserted. Michael headed upstairs, taking the steps two at a time, calling the other man's name as he went. He barreled down the hall, checking each bedroom. Every one was empty, the beds neatly made with no indication they'd been slept in the night before.

When he was sure the house was empty, he picked up the phone on a bedside table in what looked to be the master bedroom. The line was dead, not entirely unexpected. Last night's storm had also knocked out the phone service at his aunt's house.

He dug in his jeans pocket for his cell phone, clicked it on and waited for a signal. *No Service* flashed on the screen in red letters. Cursing the fickle nature of his phone's reception, he hurried down the stairs, out the rear door and into the backyard, his cell phone in hand.

Still no service.

He jogged to the front of the house as a late-model Chevrolet was pulling to the curb. He recognized Jill Coleman instantly when she got out of the car, even though her brown hair was now streaked with gray and she'd lost so much weight her dress hung on her thin figure.

She stopped dead and stood rigidly in the driveway, her face whitening as though she was looking at a ghost. At another time, Michael would tread gently, but with his cell phone still showing no service, he had no time for caution.

"Mrs. Coleman, do you have a cell phone on you?" he asked.

She gaped at him, as though appalled he dared speak to her.

"A cell phone," he repeated. "Do you have one? We need to call the police."

"The police!" That yanked her out of her stupor. She dug in the black handbag that matched her high-heeled shoes and produced a phone.

Relieved to see her phone had two bars of service, he pressed in the numbers 911.

"Why are you calling the police?" she asked.

The voice of the dispatcher came over the line, and he held up his index finger, silently asking Mrs. Coleman to wait. "I'd like to report a possible crime. I'm at the Quincy Coleman residence at 89 Oak Street. It looks like there's been a struggle."

"A struggle?" Mrs. Coleman choked out while the dispatcher asked if anybody was hurt.

"I'm not sure," he answered. "The house is empty, but there's blood on the wall."

"Blood," Mrs. Coleman repeated, then went

into motion, running awkwardly in the wet grass, her heels sinking into the mud.

"Please stay on the line—" the dispatcher began, but Michael had already clicked off the cell phone.

"Mrs. Coleman!" he yelled, giving chase.

He'd handled this all wrong. He should have calmly explained what he'd seen in the kitchen before dialing the police. A few more minutes wouldn't have mattered. There was no pressing need for an ambulance when the potential victim was missing.

Ahead of him, Mrs. Coleman was climbing the porch steps and bursting through the back door.

"Quincy!" she called.

Michael followed, catching up to her as she was surveying the chaotic scene in the kitchen. Her face was even whiter than it had been when she'd spotted him. She rushed from the kitchen to the living room, yelling her husband's name.

"He's not here, Mrs. Coleman," Michael said in a gentle voice.

She whirled on him, her manner turning from concerned to suspicious. "How do you know that?"

"I already searched the house," he said. "Upstairs and downstairs."

"What right did you have to be in the house?"

She advanced on him, her eyes wild, reminding him of the way her husband had looked at him the day before. "What were you doing here?"

He forced himself not to flinch in the face of her rage. "I needed to talk to Mr. Coleman."

"Like you talked to him yesterday? When he told you to get off his property and never come back?"

He swallowed. Even though the Colemans were separated, he should have anticipated that she'd heard about his run-in with her estranged husband.

"Why did you come back when he told you to stay away?" she demanded. "Where is he?"

A police siren sounded in the distance. Michael's stomach clenched as it dawned on him that Mrs. Coleman's tough questions weren't the only ones he'd face.

"I thought he might be more reasonable this morning than he was yesterday," he said evenly.

"What right did you have to be in our house?" she demanded again.

The volume of the police siren grew louder until it abruptly switched off. He heard the sound of car doors slamming.

"The back door was open, and I could see the kitchen was a mess," he explained. "I was afraid Mr. Coleman might be hurt so I came inside."

Mrs. Coleman's eyes narrowed as she processed the information. Footsteps pounded on the porch.

"Police!" a gruff, masculine voice yelled.

Mrs. Coleman rushed to the door, beckoning inside a middle-aged cop Michael recognized even with his hair thinning and his waist spreading. His stomach sank. Joe Wojokowski, nicknamed Wojo for short, had been the arresting officer who'd set into motion Michael's stay in juvenile detention.

"What's going on here?" Wojo asked sharply.

"I came by after church to see why Quincy wasn't there and saw *him* running from the backyard." Mrs. Coleman pointed her index finger at Michael, her expression accusatory. "He'd been in the house."

"The phones in the house are dead." Michael explained as calmly as he could. "I was trying to find a spot where I could get reception on my cell phone to call the police."

"What did you do to my husband?" Mrs. Coleman suddenly shouted.

"I didn't do anything to him." Michael addressed his next comments to Wojo. "I came by to talk to Coleman. The back door was open. I could see something wasn't right so I came into the house, but he wasn't here."

"Don't believe him! My husband warned him not to trespass." Mrs. Coleman sounded almost hysterical. "I want him arrested!"

"I had nothing to do with whatever happened here," Michael insisted, but his words had no effect.

"Arrest him!" Mrs. Coleman told Wojo. "Arrest him and make him tell you what he did to Quincy!"

Wojo walked purposefully toward Michael, producing a pair of handcuffs the way he had years ago when he'd arrested Michael inside the general store. "Put your hands out," he ordered.

"This is nuts!" Michael cried. "All I did was try to help."

"This can go easy or this can go hard," Wojo said. "It's your call, Donahue."

Surrendering to the inevitable, Michael placed his hands behind his back. The cold metal circled his wrists and the lock clicked in place while Wojo read him his rights.

"Do I at least get one phone call?" Michael asked.

Wojo gave him a little shove in the back, directing him toward the back door. "Not until we get to the station."

So much, Michael thought, for not involving Sara in his problems.

THE WHITE-HAIRED MAN ambled to where Sara waited at the front desk of the police station, his short-sleeved dress shirt partially untucked, his tie loosened, dark bags weighing down his eyes.

She briefly met his gaze, then looked away. Normally she'd greet any random stranger but she was too annoyed at being kept waiting to risk getting pulled into an idle conversation with whoever happened to walk into the police station.

"Are you the young lady who wants to see me?" The white-haired man spoke to her, his autocratic manner belying his grandfatherly appearance.

She did a double take, belatedly recognizing that he carried himself with an air of authority. "That depends on whether you're the police chief."

"I am. Name's Alton Jackson." He bowed his head but didn't offer his hand. "I usually have Sundays off. That's why I'm not in uniform."

"I'm Sara Brenneman, Michael Donahue's lawyer." She boldly stated her credentials, even though Michael hadn't formally hired her and she knew nothing about the alleged crime other than the sketchy details the desk sergeant had provided. "I want him released from custody immediately. As I understand it, there's no victim. If there's no victim, there's no crime. So you had no right to arrest him."

"Whoa. Who said Donahue was under arrest?"

"He did when he called me. He said he was read his rights and taken to the station in handcuffs."

"A misunderstanding. You're right. We're not positive there was a crime. For all we know, Quincy might have trashed his own kitchen." The skepticism in his unhurried voice told Sara he clearly didn't believe that. "Quincy's car is in his garage but he's a hiker. It's possible he had an accident in the woods. We're getting ready to comb the areas he could have reached on foot."

"Then why are you holding Michael?"

"Donahue's free to go as long as he doesn't leave town," he said, another clue that he viewed the circumstances of Coleman's disappearance as suspicious. "Officer Wojokowski and I might have a few more questions for him."

"*More* questions?" She picked up on the adjective. "You questioned him without a lawyer present?"

"He was at the scene of what might be a crime. Of course we questioned him," Chief Jackson said. "For the record, he didn't object."

Sara objected, but it was too late to mount a protest. She waited for Chief Jackson to release

Michael, wishing he'd listened when she advised him not to talk to the police. Michael eventually walked down the hall toward her, his steps heavy. He sported a day's growth of beard and droopy eyelids.

If she hadn't known better, she'd say he looked like a guilty man.

"Thanks for getting me released," he said when they were outside the station. He shielded his eyes against the sun's glare.

"It was a bogus arrest," she said through tight lips. "There's no proof against you and only circumstantial evidence of a crime."

"Then why are you ticked off?"

She didn't respond until they were both inside her car and driving away from the station. "I told you not to let them question you without a lawyer present."

The police station was located a few miles from the town's center, not far from the low point of the river where the raft tours ended. Thickly leafed trees lined the twisting road, the sun peeking through in spots to create a dappled effect, but Sara wasn't in the mood to appreciate the scenery.

"They questioned me before I called you," he said. "I don't have anything to hide so I didn't see the harm in it."

Sara could have told him the truth wasn't always an effective defense. She didn't ask where he wanted to be dropped, instead driving directly to her row house and pulling into the first vacant space along the main street. She set the parking brake. "We have things to talk about."

Her law office still smelled of paint even though she'd cracked open the windows to air it out. She led him over her splashy area rugs and past the colorful geometric abstracts she'd chosen for the walls to the indoor staircase. She didn't stop until they were upstairs in her den.

She indicated that he should sit, but she was too keyed up to settle into her sofa. He sat with his legs spread, his forearms resting on his knees.

"I need to know what happened when you got to the Coleman residence and what you told Chief Jackson," Sara began. "Don't leave out anything."

He relayed the story in a monotone voice, starting with his questionable decision to confront Coleman for a second time and the state in which he'd found the kitchen.

"Coleman was drunk yesterday," she said. "Chief Jackson said he was considering the possibility Coleman did the damage himself, then wandered off. What do you think?"

"I don't think he believes that," Michael said. "Not after the questions he asked me."

That had been Sara's impression, too. She got Michael to continue with his story, cringing when he related his encounter with Jill Coleman. "That's not good. She can make it seem like she trapped you into calling the police."

Sara paced from the wood-burning stove that would heat the room in the winter to the curio cabinet that was the same shade of red as the accent wall downstairs, trying to think of how to defend Michael if the worst happened.

"Did anyone see you last night?" she asked.

One of his hands tightened on his pant leg, his knuckles showing white. "I stayed in. Like I already told you, my aunt spent the night with a friend who had cataract surgery."

Plenty of people could have vouched for Michael's whereabouts if he'd met Sara and the Pollocks at the Blue Haven, but pointing that out would be fruitless.

"It's vital you don't talk to the police again without a lawyer present," she said. "You don't need a criminal lawyer just yet, but I have a contact who can recommend some names. It won't hurt to be prepared."

"You mean in case Coleman's dead and I'm charged with the crime?" he asked bluntly.

"Well, yes," Sara said.

He straightened and crossed his arms over his

chest, his mouth thinning, his eyes narrowing. "Aren't you going to ask me where he is?"

"Excuse me?"

A muscle jumped in his jaw. "As you pointed out, I was seen running from the scene of the crime. You've been in town long enough to know that Coleman's a respected citizen. Nobody besides me has a motive. So go ahead. Ask me."

Sara wasn't sure what was going on. His voice was thick with emotion, his face pinched with it.

"I get it," he said when she didn't respond. "A good lawyer never asks a client if he's guilty because she's afraid of the answer."

She took a few steps closer to him, refusing to be intimidated by the tension radiating from him.

"There are so many things wrong with what you just said I don't know where to begin, but I'll give it a try." She ticked off the points on her fingers. "One, you're not officially my client. Two, where's the victim if you were running from the scene of the crime? And three, I don't need to ask you anything to know you're not guilty."

The tight arch of his shoulders seemed to relax, but only slightly. "How do you know?"

That was like asking how she knew the sky was blue. Or that birds could fly. Or flowers bloom.

"I don't only believe you, Michael, I believe *in* you." In the absolute silence that followed she realized what she'd admitted and swallowed a groan. "Though don't go getting any ideas because the offer's off the table. Whatever was brewing between us, it's over. I'm not interested anymore."

His only reaction was a slow nod. "That's smart. I'm not the right guy for you."

"I agree. It will never work out between us, so I have no more interest in a personal relationship." She deliberately used strong, definitive language, not wanting him to mistake her position. "Anything between us from now on will be strictly business so you can stop avoiding me."

He didn't bother to deny he'd stayed away from the Blue Haven last night because of her. "Okay."

"That's settled then." She made a snap decision, refusing to give herself time for second-guessing. "But we *are* having dinner together tonight."

His brow wrinkled. "You're not making sense."

"I should have said we're having dinner together if the police don't find Coleman," she said. "By tonight, every local in town will know the police questioned you in Coleman's disappearance. You'll need to show your face to prove you have nothing to hide. And I need to make sure you don't do or say anything you shouldn't."

He took his time before nodding his silent agreement, his gray-blue eyes fastened on her. She'd provided a perfectly legitimate reason why they should have dinner, but as attraction flared inside her, she realized Michael wouldn't be the one with something to hide tonight.

She would be.

CHAPTER TEN

WORD HAD gotten around Indigo Springs that Quincy Coleman was missing and Michael was a suspect, just as Sara had predicted.

That could be the only explanation for the stares they received that evening as Michael followed Sara and an unfamiliar hostess through Angelo's Italian Restaurant to the outdoor seating area.

The clientele consisted mostly of tourists, few of whom paid attention to their entrance, but the locals strained their necks to get a good look at him. Michael kept his back straight and held his head high, pretending he didn't notice the faces from his past. A former teacher. The clerk at the post office. The police chief who'd questioned him that afternoon.

"You sure you want to eat outside?" the young, pretty hostess asked when they were on a covered patio decorated with tiny white lights and potted plants. A ceiling fan whirred overhead. "It's warm even with the fan."

Only one other couple had opted for alfresco dining, a fit-looking pair in their twenties who were probably taking hiking and biking trips along the Lehigh.

"We're sure," Michael said.

He picked up a menu after the hostess seated them, although he'd rather look at Sara. She wore an unlawyerlike short skirt and a tight-fitting shirt with a wide V-neck. The deep purple of the shirt should have clashed with the reddish highlights in her hair, but didn't. She looked fantastic.

He reminded himself that their arrangement was strictly business. She'd made it clear that whatever personal interest she'd had in him was gone, for which he could only blame himself, but he'd give anything if they were a normal couple and this was a real date.

"They still haven't found that retired banker." The voice of the other woman on the patio carried to their table, slamming Michael back to reality. "I heard it wasn't random. Some guy had a grudge against him."

"Then he's probably dead," her male companion said. "The asshole probably killed him."

So much for thinking anything about tonight

could be normal. The hell of it was Michael couldn't even defend himself. If he corrected the woman's misconception about who held the grudge, he'd only succeed in drawing more attention to himself. He tried to focus on the menu offerings, but the print ran together.

"Don't let it get to you," Sara told him in a quiet voice. "She's a tourist. She doesn't know what she's talking about."

"She had to hear it from somewhere," he said.

"There's always gossip when something like this happens," Sara said. "The people who know you don't think you're guilty."

"Some of them do." Michael nodded in the direction of Alton Jackson, who was striding onto the outdoor patio with the vigor of a man half his age. Michael supposed it was too much to hope the police chief would leave them alone.

"Ms. Brenneman, Donahue." Jackson nodded to one of the extra seats at their table for four. "Can I sit down?"

"Certainly," Sara said.

The police chief's white hair was a dead giveaway that he was approaching retirement age, but his eyes were clear and his manner commanding. He settled himself into the chair, then rested his forearms on the table. His voice was too soft for the other couple on the patio to hear, but discretion was probably unnecessary. The man was signing a credit-card slip and the woman had moved on to a loud one-way discussion of her exercise regimen.

"I expect you heard Coleman's still missing," Chief Jackson said. "We searched the woods in back of his house today but didn't find him. We'll widen the search area come daybreak but it's looking less and less likely he wandered off on his own."

The police chief looked pointedly at Michael, who met his gaze, reminding himself he had nothing to hide. Jackson had made no secret of his dislike for Michael, but the chief had a reputation for being thorough and honest. If a crime had been committed, he wouldn't pin the blame on Michael without proof.

"Kenny Grieb heard you arguing with Quincy the day before he disappeared," the chief said.

"That's no secret," Michael said, disliking the direction of the conversation. "I already told you about the argument."

The chief's gaze didn't waver from his face. "You didn't tell me you threatened to kill him."

"What?" Michael exclaimed. The heads of the tourist couple, who'd risen from their table, snapped in their direction. Michael waited until they left the patio before he continued. "That's not true. I didn't say that."

"So you didn't tell Quincy you were tired of the way he was treating you?"

Michael searched his memory, futilely trying to recall his exact words. "I might have said something like that, but I swear I never threatened him."

"Did any of the other neighbors who witnessed the argument say they heard a threat?" Sara asked, as coolly and calmly as if she were cross-examining a witness in a courtroom.

"None of those neighbors were at the house next door," the chief said, in effect providing the answer. Kenny was their only witness. Kenny, who'd disliked Michael since they were in their teens.

"I don't care what Kenny says he heard, it didn't happen," Michael said. "Any bad blood between Coleman and me was on his part, not mine."

"That may be," the police chief said slowly, "but I can imagine how a man could get tired of so much ill will being directed his way."

The legs of the chair made a scraping noise as Chief Jackson pushed back from the table and stood. He bent down, still speaking in that same quiet voice. "You better hope we find Quincy alive and well, Donahue."

"And you better have solid evidence before you make a move or you'll find yourself facing a claim of false arrest," Sara replied in an equally soft voice.

Chief Jackson's jaw tightened before he left them with an insincere sounding, "Enjoy your dinner."

Even as the police chief retreated, Michael's muscles coiled in what he recognized as the fight or flight instinct. He was leaning toward flight, not only from this restaurant, but from this miserable town.

"If you leave," Sara said, as though she'd read his mind, "you'll look guilty."

He couldn't tell by her impassive delivery whether the chief's visit had caused her to doubt him. His stomach clenched. He couldn't stand it if she believed he'd threatened to kill Coleman.

"Grieb is trying to make trouble for me," Michael said.

"I picked up on that. The same way I figured out Chief Jackson is stirring things up to see if anything shakes loose." She put an elbow on the table and rested her chin in her hand. "Any particular reason he doesn't like you?"

Michael wished he didn't have to tell her, that he could pretend he'd never done anything to raise the ire of the Indigo Springs police. One thing he'd never been, though, was a liar.

"Did you notice the general store a couple of doors down from the restaurant?"

"Abe's?"

"That's the one." He picked up his water glass, put it back down again. "I got arrested for breaking and entering when I was seventeen and did four months in juvenile detention."

The space between her brows crinkled. She stared at him so hard he felt like she was trying to see inside him. "I can't picture you doing something like that."

The idea to jimmy the lock and break into the store hadn't been Michael's, but shifting the blame hadn't been an option then and wasn't now. "I was no angel. I had some priors for vandalism, shoplifting, fighting, that kind of thing."

"Was this after your mother died?" she asked.

"Before and after," he said, unwilling to use his mother's death as an excuse. "But lots of kids lose a parent and don't get into the trouble I did."

"There's something I don't understand," she said. "Why did you move in with your great-aunt after your mother died? Why not stay with your father?"

"I don't know who my father is." He'd never spoken the words aloud before. To anyone.

Now that he had, the rest of the story tumbled free. "My mother didn't know, either. She had a drug problem and used to have these black-outs. It was years before I figured out I was conceived during one of them."

Michael was almost afraid to look into Sara's eyes to gauge her reaction to his dark secret, but he saw compassion instead of censure. "How did she die?"

"A cocaine overdose. In the middle of the afternoon." He'd come home from school that day, pleased to see his mother's car in the driveway so he wouldn't have to wait to tell her he'd aced his algebra test. "She was just lying there on the coach, not moving. There were lines of white powder on the coffee table. I knew she was already gone, but I kept shaking her and shaking her."

His voice trailed off, the horror of that afternoon reaching out from the past and grabbing him. Sara stretched her hand across the table and laid it on his arm. It was warm and soft…and comforting. "I'm sorry."

"Me, too." He smiled sadly. "She wasn't the best mom, but she made sure I knew she loved me."

"The police should have cut you a break when you got in trouble instead of sending you to juvenile detention," she said.

"I never blamed them for arresting me," he said, then stated the credo he'd come to live by. "A man has to take responsibility for his actions."

"But you were a boy."

"I was seventeen, six months from being a legal adult." Michael had been two months shy of his eighteenth birthday when he got out of juvenile detention, two months in which he'd taken up with Chrissy and become increasingly unwelcome in his aunt's house. "I should have known better."

"You couldn't have—?"

"I'm sorry I haven't taken your order yet." A redhead Michael recognized from the wedding appeared at the table. He dredged up her boyfriend's name. Chase Bradford. Yes, that was it. "I'm Mandy, and I'll be your server to…"

The waitress's voice trailed off, her eyes lighting on Sara and growing unfriendly. "Oh, it's you."

"Hello, Mandy," Sara said with a smile that seemed forced.

The waitress scowled and positioned her pen over her order pad, focusing on Michael. "What can I get you?"

"Why don't you order first, Sara?" Michael suggested, earning him a grateful smile from Sara and more frostiness from the waitress.

"What was that all about?" Michael asked after they'd placed twin orders for the house specialty of chicken marsala over spaghetti. The hostess was seating more diners on the patio, with a few of the new arrivals slanting Michael curious looks, but nobody aiming as much dislike at him as Mandy had directed at Sara.

"As near as I can tell, she's unhappy I didn't hire her as my office manager," Sara said. "Could we talk about something else?"

"You mean besides missing men, suspicious police chiefs and surly waitresses? Hmm." Michael pretended to mull it over. "Works for me."

She laughed, and the light, melodic sound seemed like an invitation to put his troubles aside, at least for tonight. After a moment, he found himself laughing with her.

SARA HAD the warm, excited feeling of a woman on a good date with a man who intrigued her.

She could track the moment their business arrangement started to feel like a date back to her laugh. As the outdoor patio filled up, she and Michael had discussed typical date topics: travel, books, music.

"Tuareg Blues? Never heard of them," she said when they were outside the restaurant, pleasantly full from a delicious meal. "Have they been on tour?"

He chuckled. "Tuareg blues isn't a band—it's a style of African music. The Tuareg are one of the ethnic groups that live in Niger. Their music is hard to explain, but it's kind of like desert blues."

They walked through town toward Sara's place, as they'd done the first night they'd met, passing the same shops, their shoulders occasionally brushing because the sidewalk was too narrow. Michael had been a mystery to Sara then, and it occurred to her she didn't know him much better now.

His life in Niger had come up during the dinner conversation, but not in any depth. She hadn't questioned him about the Peace Corps, perhaps because of Johnny Pollock's deluded request to talk Michael out of volunteering for another two years. Now it seemed silly not to ask. "What did you do for the Peace Corps while you were in Niger?"

"Helped a crew in one of the villages build a cement schoolhouse," he said. "Cement is a big deal over there. The old school buildings never last through the rainy season because they're made of mud brick walls and millet stalk roofs."

"It seems to me I remember hearing what a poor country Niger is," she said.

"One of the poorest in the world. Most of the time it's hot, dry and dusty. The village where I lived didn't have electricity or telephones or even running water."

She could hardly imagine a world without indoor showers. "Then how did you bathe?"

"Well water," he said. "I got pretty good at taking a bucket bath."

"It sounds like a tough place to live," she said.

"It's tough for the people who are born there," he said. "Life expectancy is somewhere around forty-five."

Her hand flew to her mouth, horror filling her at the number he'd cited. "Why so low?"

"Lots of reasons. High child mortality. Poor health care. Ignorance about how to stop disease from spreading."

She looked up, surprised to realize they were in view of her home. She should tell him goodnight and go upstairs, but she wanted to know more about what made him tick.

She sat down on the park bench overlooking the street and the small park from where Ben Smith had aimed his slingshot two nights before. Wordlessly, Michael joined her, the brush of his arm against hers sending a tingle down her body.

She reminded herself that Michael had repeatedly proved he wasn't relationship material, and she'd accepted that and moved on. It shouldn't matter that he felt compelled to volunteer to work in the world's poorest countries, but God help her, it did.

"Niger must be a depressing place," she remarked.

"It's not," he said. "That's the amazing thing. The people have so little yet they're warm and generous with what they do have. And happy, too."

"How about you, Michael? Does the Peace Corps life make you happy?"

"Happy enough," he said, but there was a certain weariness in his voice.

"Johnny says most Peace Corps volunteers only serve two years but you've already given six." She cut her eyes at him, watching him carefully. "He says you got offered an assignment in Ghana, but he's not sure you should take it. He thinks you're burned out."

"Johnny talks too much."

"*Are* you burned out?" she prompted.

"It wouldn't matter if I was. It's what I do." He stared down at his hands for long seconds before he lifted his head and looked at her. "I need to balance the bad things I've done in my life with something good."

"The bad things?"

"Chrissy." He sucked in a breath, and she could tell he was wrestling with strong emotions. "I'm finding out that no matter how much good I do, I can never make up for what happened to her."

Ah, now she understood. "No wonder Johnny asked for help in convincing you to leave the Peace Corps."

"Is that what you're trying to do?"

"Of course not. Yet he has this wild idea I can get you to move back to Indigo Springs. He doesn't understand I'm the last person who can convince you of anything."

He blinked, seeming surprised by her statement. "Nobody can get me to move back here, but you could convince me of a great many other things."

"Then I wish I could convince you to see yourself like I see you," she said.

"And how's that?" he asked.

She'd promised not to let herself be vulnerable to him again, but the answer was too important. "I see a man who cares about the world around him. A man who should forgive himself for the mistakes he made when he was a teenager."

His expression softened, something that resembled awe entering his eyes. He reached up and touched her cheek before his fingers glided softly over her lips.

"What are you doing?" she asked, her lips moving against his fingertips.

Laughter rang out down the block. Two young couples, probably tourists soaking in the atmosphere and the architecture, came into view.

"Before I saw those people coming," he said, surprise in his voice, "I'm pretty sure I was going to kiss you."

"What makes you think I'd let you? I thought we got it straight this afternoon that the offer's off the table." She tried to make her voice stern but failed miserably. "Once spurned, twice shy."

"You think I spurned you?" He captured one of her hands in his. "I've never wanted any woman the way I want you."

"You have a strange way of showing it."

"It's not that simple, Sara. I've already told you. I can't let you pay for what I've done."

"So random people in town, like Quincy Coleman, get to decide what's best for us?" she challenged. "We don't get any say?"

He frowned. "It sounds wrong when you put it that way."

"It is wrong. This isn't about anybody else. It's about you and me and what we want." She almost groaned. She'd decided to keep things between them strictly business. What was the matter with her that she couldn't stick to her resolution? "Forget I said that. There is no you and me."

"Are you sure about that?" he asked, still holding her hand, effortlessly reestablishing the charged connection between them with the softness of his question. "Because what I want is you."

She searched his eyes, saw her own desire reflected in them and let go of her wounded pride. Michael wasn't like the other men who'd come and gone in her life, having such a shallow impression of her that she could barely remember some of their names. Something about him touched her so deeply she couldn't pretend that this wasn't what she wanted.

That *he* wasn't what she wanted.

"Sara?" he prompted, sounding unsure of himself, as though afraid she'd decided against him.

That hint of uncertainty put her all the way over the edge.

"I want you, too," she whispered.

MICHAEL FELT as though the weight that had been pressing down on him had lifted. So many people in his life had been ready to believe the worst of him it seemed a miracle that Sara only believed the best.

He'd tried to stay away from her because he feared she might suffer repercussions, but so far his fears had proved groundless. Because of her faith, he wanted to believe that she was right, that they were the only two people in their relationship who mattered.

So he did.

They were inside the office he'd painted, with the red accent wall and other unexpected splashes of color which infused it with a sense of style. She was almost to the foot of the stairs when she glanced back at him. He braced himself, half expecting her to say she'd changed her mind, but she smiled at him. The smile was full not of doubt but invitation.

"You should have waited until we were upstairs to look at me like that," he said.

She turned the entire way around, her grin even wider, even more enticing. "Why's that?"

"Because now we won't make it there." He pulled her to him, his arms wrapping around her, his mouth coming down on hers. He felt the urgency well up inside him, as though it had been buried beneath the surface and finally set free.

Everything about her excited him. The smell of the citrusy soap on her skin and the hint of flowers in her hair. The vague taste of the wine she'd had at dinner on her tongue. The sexy little moans she made deep in her throat. And the smooth, lithe feel of her skin.

Blood roared in his ears, drowning out sound, but he could feel his heart beating hard. Or was that her heart pounding against his chest?

He put a hand at the small of her back, molding her lower body to his, soundlessly communicating how much he wanted her. He backed her up against the wall nearest the stairs, kissing her mouth, then her breast through the thin fabric of her purple top. He unhooked her bra, and she lifted her arms, enabling him to slip off her shirt so she was naked from the waist up.

He'd told the unembroidered truth about never wanting any woman the way he did her. He couldn't remember this desperate need to join with a woman, this absolute sense of rightness when she was in his arms.

He kissed a trail down her neck and over her breastbone before reaching one of her small, perfect breasts. His mouth fastened on a nipple.

He sucked and heard another of those sexy moans, this one louder than the others.

He brought his mouth back to hers, his tongue mating with her tongue. When she reached between them and stroked his hard length through his khakis, he nearly lost control. He reached under her skirt, cupping her rear end, bringing her more fully against him.

"A condom. In my purse," she said, her sentences fragmented. "Put…it on."

Out of the corner of his eye, he spied her purse on the floor, the contents spilled over the gleaming hardwood.

He lifted his head. He was breathing hard, his chest moving up and down in ragged gasps. Now that they'd reached the pivotal moment, he wanted her desperately, even more than he wanted to leave Indigo Springs, but there was a question he needed to ask. "Are *you* sure?"

"I swear, Michael." Her voice was steadier now but just as breathless as his. "If you stop now, I'll have to hurt you."

He smiled, further turned on by her eagerness. "I'm not sure I could stop."

"Then don't," she said.

Somehow, between kisses, her panties disappeared and he sheathed himself. Then she was guiding him inside her, gasping as he filled her.

She clung to him, her legs wrapping around his waist, her back plastered against the wall.

It vaguely occurred to Michael that they might not have picked the easiest position for lovemaking, but then she moved with him and sensation inundated him. It was the same as when they'd kissed, as though they'd made love a hundred times instead of this once.

He felt the first spasms start to shake her and tried to make it last for her, but then her inner muscles contracted around him, and he came, too, the world shattering around him yet somehow making him feel whole.

They held each other after it was over, their skin damp, their breathing slowly returning to normal. He leaned his forehead against hers, content to remain as close as two people could be.

"Wow," she said on a sigh.

Happiness filled him, more acute since it had been so long since he'd felt it in the purest form. He kissed her lingeringly on the mouth. "I knew it would be like this between us."

"Me, too," she said.

"But I have to be straight with you." He drew back, not wanting to break the mood but knowing he had to. "All I can offer you is a short-term affair. You know that, don't you?"

"Don't worry, Michael. I know this can't

last." Sara took a breath before she continued. "I wouldn't have invited you upstairs if I couldn't handle that."

"You still want me upstairs?"

"I still want you." She deliberately glanced at the articles of her clothing that were still on the floor. "It doesn't seem to matter if it's upstairs or downstairs."

He laughed, then moved away from her and helped her pick up her clothes. They ascended the stairs together, Michael holding Sara's hand securely, already wishing the time wasn't soon approaching when he'd have to let her go.

CHAPTER ELEVEN

A RAY OF SUNLIGHT peeked through an opening in the mini-blinds of Sara's bedroom window and bathed her face in light, pulling her out of a satisfied sleep.

Her body still languid from last night's love-making, she stretched her arms overhead, smiled and opened her eyes. Her smile disappeared.

The other side of the bed was empty.

"Michael," she called, thinking he might be in the bathroom.

Silence.

He was gone.

She smoothed a hand over the rumpled sheets, finding them cool to the touch; he'd been gone for a while.

She smothered her disappointment. It was better this way. She'd delayed the official opening of her practice until later in the week but Laurie would be arriving soon, as well as the delivery men with some office furniture she'd ordered. Now that the walls were painted, she and Laurie planned to put the finishing touches on the office.

Sara didn't have time to linger in bed with a man who hadn't even bothered to leave a note, no matter how sexy he was and how much she wanted him.

The phone on her bedside table rang. She leaned over and picked it up on the first ring. "Hello?"

"Good morning." Michael's voice glided over her, the way his hands had the night before. She instantly forgave him for that note he hadn't left. "I'm sorry I didn't say goodbye."

He'd left Indigo Springs.

If she'd been hooked up to a heart monitor, the machine would show a flat line. She could barely think, let alone talk. Just last night he'd told her he was only in town for the short term and reiterated he could never make Indigo Springs his home.

How could she protest when she'd assured him she could handle a fling?

But there was another reason he shouldn't have left town, one not involving her.

"How am I going to explain this to Chief Jackson?" she finally choked out.

"Chief Jackson?" He sounded puzzled. "Even if he saw me leaving your place, it's none of his business."

Now that she was over the shock of hearing him say goodbye, her mind started to work again. Cell-phone reception in the mountains was spotty, and their connection was clear, as though he was speaking from a landline.

"Where are you?" she asked.

"My aunt's house." A pause. "Where did you think I was?"

She closed her eyes. He'd been apologizing for leaving her *bed,* not for leaving *town.* Her heartbeat slowed down, and her airways opened up, the strangling sensation easing.

"Never mind." She cleared her throat and said what a woman who could handle a fling would say. "There's no need to apologize. No strings, remember?"

There couldn't be any ties. One day soon both his aunt's problems and the mystery of Quincy Coleman's disappearance would be solved, and Michael would be gone for good.

She'd known that going in. Now she had to get herself to accept it.

"What are your plans for today?" he asked.

For the first time, Sara looked at the bedside

clock. She'd overslept. Laurie was due to arrive in forty-five minutes.

"Getting ready for business," she said. "How about you?"

"I ran into Johnny when I stopped for coffee. He's gonna help search for Coleman so I thought I would, too."

"No!" Sara sat straight up in bed, pushing her hair out of her face, desperate to convince him to listen to her. "You can't help, Michael. Think what the chief would make of it if you found a body."

"But what if Coleman isn't dead? What if he did have a hiking accident? He could be out there hurt somewhere."

"If somebody killed him and you find him, the chief will say you knew where to look."

"I won't be alone, Sara. I'll be with Johnny."

"That won't matter to the chief," she argued.

"That's a risk I'm willing to take." He sounded as though her very real, bluntly stated concerned hadn't swayed him in the slightest.

"But why? Explain the logic in this to me."

"I spent a lot of time in the woods when I lived with my aunt. I know some spots others might not check."

She heard the determination in his voice and couldn't help admiring him for listening to his conscience, even if his sense of right and wrong was steering him down a potentially disastrous path.

"I'm still strongly advising against it," she said.

"That's the second reason I'm glad I'm not officially your client."

"What's the first?"

"Lawyers don't make love with their clients." His voice lowered a full octave, sending shivers over her skin. "If I were your client, I would have missed the best sex of my life."

She felt herself smile. "Are you trying to distract me, Michael Donahue?"

"Guilty as charged," he said. "I've been distracted all morning thinking about what we did last night and wondering how soon we can do it again."

A languorous warmth spread through her body, and she could almost feel his hands on her, the hard length of him completing her. "You're not playing fair. I haven't even gotten out of bed yet."

His voice got even lower. "I wish I was still in bed with you."

She whimpered. "If you're trying to seduce me, you're doing a good job of it."

"I'll do even better tonight," he said. "I'll bring takeout so you can build up your strength before we start."

She was smiling when she disconnected the phone call until it occurred to her that Michael's distraction had worked to perfection.

She'd forgotten all about talking him out of searching for Quincy Coleman.

LAURIE FINISHED setting up the fax machine and tackled the box of files Sara had set on her desk.

The delivery men had arrived promptly at nine o'clock, bringing the boxy loveseats and chairs Sara had chosen for the reception area. They were a burnt-orange color with bright-red touches that picked up the shade of the accent wall and the boss's personality.

For the balance of the morning, she and Sara had worked diligently to bring character to the office with decorations they lugged from upstairs.

Colorful carpet runners. Plaques. Avant-garde prints. Law-office chic, Laurie called it.

They'd kept so busy Laurie had managed not to blurt out she'd slept with Kenny on Saturday. The fact that lovemaking with her ex wasn't an appropriate workplace topic didn't stop her. Her confusion did. What would she say if Sara asked how she felt about what she'd done?

Terrible?

Wonderful?

Stupid?

The truth was probably all of the above. Laurie would have felt even more dim-witted if she'd spent the night with Kenny instead of leaving as soon as the power came back on.

She needed time to think, which was the extent of what she'd told him.

Not about whether she was still in love with him, which had never been in question, but about whether he could ever be more in love with her than with the memory of Chrissy Coleman.

"Hello. Anybody here?"

Laurie stood up from where she'd been crouching beside the file cabinet. A fresh-faced teenage girl, her blond hair tied back from her face, stood on one of the new carpet runners holding a white paper bag.

"Delivery from Angelo's," she announced and checked the slip attached to the bag. "One vegetarian calzone and one meatball sub."

"Sounds delicious." Sara appeared from the back room, waving off Laurie's attempt to extract her wallet from her purse. She handed some bills to the young girl. "I had dinner at Angelo's just last night."

"I remember seeing you on the patio with that hot guy," the girl said, piquing Laurie's curiosity. What hot guy? "Mandy was your waitress, right?"

"Right," Sara said.

"She's supposed to be working the lunch shift today, but she called in sick." The girl looked around, as though somebody might overhear her gossiping. "She had a miscarriage last night."

"Oh, no," Laurie said, her hands going to either side of her face. She remembered only too well the frightening cramps that had preceded her own miscarriage, the devastation when she lost the baby. It had signaled the beginning of the end of her marriage. "How is she?"

"She's tough," the girl said, "so I'm sure she'll be okay."

"How are you?" Sara asked the instant the delivery girl was gone, her eyes soft with compassion, making Laurie glad she'd confided in her boss about the past.

"Okay. All the pain came rushing back for a moment, but my miscarriage was a long time ago." Laurie sighed, unwilling to examine her feelings in depth or to admit she still yearned for a baby. She wasn't ready to figure out if her longing was for Kenny's baby. "Come on, let's talk about something else. Like your hot guy. Let me take a guess. Mike Donahue?"

"It's not what you think." Sara's face flushed, telling Laurie it was exactly what she thought.

"We only went to dinner so he could show his face in town and prove he had nothing to hide."

Laurie carried her meatball sub to the reception area, sat down in one of the orange chairs and popped the top of her diet soda while Sara did the same.

"What would he have to hide?" Laurie asked.

Sara paused in the act of bringing her calzone to her mouth. "You haven't heard about Quincy Coleman?"

"What about Quincy Coleman?" Laurie said.

Sara put her lunch back on the wrapper. "He's been missing since Sunday morning. It's possible he had a hiking accident but the police don't think so. His kitchen was a mess. Smashed bottles and plates. Overturned chairs. A streak of blood."

"How did I miss this?" Laurie figured out the reason on her own: She'd been distracted with thoughts of Kenny. "Do the police have any suspects?"

"Only one—Michael. They say he was tired of Coleman constantly demeaning him."

"That's ridiculous!" Laurie exclaimed. "The Mike I knew in high-school wasn't vindictive. I can't believe he's changed that much."

"He hasn't," Sara said. "He's completely innocent."

"Then why do the police think he's guilty?"

Sara wrapped her hand around her soda can but didn't pick it up. "I take it you haven't talked to Kenny this weekend."

Laurie's breath caught and she had to will herself to exhale. "What does Kenny have to do with it?"

"Quite a lot. He claims he overheard Michael threaten to kill Coleman."

"When was this?"

"Saturday afternoon."

Yet on Saturday night Kenny hadn't mentioned Mike Donahue to Laurie, not that they'd done much talking.

"Some other people also heard the argument," Sara continued. "Kenny's the only one who reported the threat."

"You don't believe Kenny, do you?" Laurie asked.

"Michael said it didn't happen. So no, I don't."

The scent of meatballs reached Laurie's nostrils, and her stomach turned over, her appetite gone. Even without all the details, she believed Michael over Kenny, too.

"Are you okay?" Sara placed her hand over Laurie's, her expression concerned. "I didn't mean to upset you."

"Don't apologize," Laurie said. "You just knocked some sense into me."

MICHAEL LAY on the soft mattress of the queen-size bed with his eyes wide open, but it was so dark in Sara's bedroom he could barely make out the shape of the ceiling fan.

He should be weary from a long day spent traipsing through the woods, futilely searching for any sign of Quincy Coleman. But now that Sara was asleep, the mystery turned over and over in his mind.

He hadn't thought about much except Sara when she was awake. He'd arrived earlier that evening bearing takeout deli sandwiches and a rented DVD, but they hadn't gotten around to watching the movie.

They'd entertained each other much more enjoyably in bed.

They hadn't talked much about Quincy Coleman, either, which could be why thoughts of the man buzzed in his brain. The longer Michael stayed awake, the less likely it seemed that Coleman had been the victim of foul play.

The man had been well on his way to getting falling-down drunk Saturday afternoon. The empty beer cans in the garage, the bloodshot eyes and the slurred speech left that in no dispute.

The whiskey bottles in Coleman's kitchen strongly suggested he'd kept on drinking after Michael had left. Yes, there'd been blood on the wall but not much. Coleman could have cut himself on a broken piece of glass after anger got the best of him.

It made more sense that he had gone into the woods to blow off steam than that someone had killed him and taken away the body. When the heavy rains came, it was easy to imagine Coleman getting hit by a fallen tree branch or tripping and injuring himself.

The problem with Michael's theory was that the police had considered it, too. Search teams had scoured the area Coleman could have reached on foot and found nothing.

On foot.

The two words jumped out at Michael, bringing him even more fully awake. Coleman's Cadillac was still parked in his garage, but it didn't necessarily follow that Coleman had been on foot.

Not when Michael clearly remembered his surprise at seeing a second vehicle in that garage: An off-road motorcycle.

He sat up and swung his legs off the bed, groping in the darkness for his clothes on the floor. If Coleman was on the motorbike, the search teams hadn't covered a wide enough area. He pulled on his jeans and shirt, dressing as quickly as he could manage.

"Michael?" Sara's sleepy voice penetrated

the quiet darkness. The glowing red numbers on her bedside alarm clock showed it was well past midnight. "Where are you going?"

She'd probably try to talk him into waiting until morning if he confessed his destination was Coleman's garage.

"I'm leaving now," he whispered, "but I'll see you tomorrow. You're coming over to give Aunt Felicia an update, right?"

"I don't have anything to tell her yet. I need to contact more lenders." Her voice was heavy with sleep, her sentences barely comprehensible. She seemed completely vulnerable, totally trusting. Of him.

Tenderness rose up inside him. He walked to the opposite side of the bed, sat down on the edge of the mattress and kissed her.

Her arms came around him, her soft, pliant lips molding sweetly to his, the sleepy feel of her making him want her all over again.

"You don't have to go," she said when he lifted his mouth.

Yet he did. As much as he wanted to stay here in Sara's bedroom and let himself tumble into love with her, he couldn't pretend they were a normal couple or that these were normal circumstances.

"Yes, I do." He kissed her again, swiftly so

he wouldn't yield to his desire to crawl back under the sheets. "Go back to sleep."

The town was as sleepy as Sara, with few cars on the street and little noise except for the cries of night birds, crickets and tree frogs. He turned off Main Street, and the night seemed to get even quieter. With the windows of his PT Cruiser open, he could hear the whisper of the wind rustling the leaves in the trees.

The night was overcast, the clouds blocking out the moon, with only the headlights of Michael's car and those of another vehicle maybe a half mile behind him shining through the darkness.

Michael changed his mind about pulling up in front of Coleman's house and parked a block away as a precaution. Moving quickly and silently, he walked down the street and around the house to the detached garage.

The sliding garage door had four window panels across the top, high enough that it wasn't necessary to stoop. Michael peered inside, saw only blackness and immediately regretted that he hadn't brought a flashlight.

Cursing under his breath, he moved to a window panel closer to where the motorbike had been parked but still saw nothing.

He headed for the side entrance door, holding his breath as he twisted the knob. Bingo. It was unlocked.

Light bathed him before he could pull the door open.

"Freeze and put your hands where I can see them."

He recognized Wojokowski's voice and silently cursed himself for letting this happen even as he obeyed the police officer. But how had Wojo caught him? He hadn't been on Coleman's property long enough for the police to respond even if a neighbor had spotted him and called it in.

"Now turn around," Wojo ordered.

Michael turned, the flare of the flashlight shining into his eyes and causing his pupils to contract. He shielded his eyes with a hand.

"It's not what you think," he said.

"I'll be the judge of that," Wojo said. "You got three seconds to tell me what you're doing here."

Michael quickly explained about the motorbike he'd seen in the garage and his theory that Coleman might have been riding it the night he disappeared. Wojo listened silently, then ordered him to stand against the wall of the garage while he frisked him.

"Your story sounds like a crock of shit," he said.

"Aren't you even going to check it out?"

Wojo pulled open the side entrance door and swept the powerful beam of his flashlight over the interior of the garage. The aluminum frame of the motorbike reflected the light back at them. Michael's stomach did a free fall.

"Like I said, a crock of shit," Wojo said. "I could arrest you for trespassing, but we'll be arresting you for something a whole lot more serious soon enough. So why don't you save us a lot of trouble and just tell me where Quincy is?"

"I don't know," Michael said tightly.

"I got to hand it to you, Donahue. You sound convincing. You using that same innocent act on that pretty lawyer? Is that how you got her to sleep with you?"

"Leave her out of this," Michael bit out, wondering how Wojo could possibly know about Sara.

"I didn't bring her into it," he said. "You better get out of here while the gettin's good, Donahue."

Michael retraced his path, passing within steps of a generic four-door automobile that hadn't been parked in front of Coleman's house ten minutes ago. He recognized it for what it was: an unmarked police car.

Wojo's comment about Sara suddenly made sense.

The policeman knew Michael was sleeping with Sara because he'd been following him.

SARA'S HEART raced and her legs pumped as she ran, her long, gliding strides carrying her around the high-school track that the receptionist at the dentist's office next door had recommended.

The track was considerably flatter than the hilly three-mile course she usually ran in the mornings and also much quieter. The only other person in sight was a lone woman standing at the opposite end of the oval.

Sara slowed to a jog and then to a walk, her body flushed with the natural high she often got from running. Although today she couldn't swear that her morning run was the cause of her euphoria.

The more likely reason for that was Michael Donahue.

The pure and simple truth was that he made her happy. Her life made sense since they'd started sleeping together two nights ago, as though he'd filled the last piece of emptiness inside her. She wrapped her arms around herself as she cooled down, hugging the knowledge to herself. She refused to think about what the future would bring.

For now, she was just going to be happy.

The track made a loop around the high-school football field, with goal posts positioned on either end. Sara rounded one of the curves, closing the distance between herself and the woman. She placed the woman's age at about sixty. She was dressed in low-heeled shoes and a navy dress too dark for the sunny day.

What was she doing here? Sara wondered. She obviously hadn't come to exercise.

"Good morning," Sara called to her.

The woman had been standing still but now went into motion, walking directly toward Sara. Thin and pale and graying, she looked as though a strong wind might blow her over. She clutched what appeared to be envelopes tied together with a pink ribbon.

"Are you Sara Brenneman?" she asked.

"I am." Sara came to a stop, her breathing only just now returning to normal. "How did you know that?"

"I went to your office. Nobody was there yet the receptionist next door told me where to find you," the woman said. "I'm Jill Coleman, Quincy's wife."

So that was the reason for the woman's frazzled appearance. Somebody had told Sara the couple hadn't lived together in years, but Jill Coleman obviously still cared for her estranged husband. Sara temporarily shoved aside her curiosity over why the woman had gone to such lengths to seek her out.

"I'm sorry about what you're going through," Sara said. "Is there any news about your husband?"

"None," Mrs. Coleman said.

"Well, I hope they find him soon." Sara waited, her mind rewinding to the visit Jill Coleman's husband had paid her a week ago today. She'd also been dressed in running clothes that day. She got the uneasy feeling this confrontation wouldn't go any better than that one had.

Mrs. Coleman moistened her lips. "I hear you're Michael Donahue's lawyer."

Sara swallowed a sigh. On some level she'd known this was about Michael. "I'm his great-aunt's lawyer. Michael doesn't have a lawyer because he hasn't done anything to warrant one."

"Chief Jackson told me you got Donahue released after the police arrested him."

"Michael was never under arrest," Sara said.

"If you hadn't interfered," Mrs. Coleman countered, "the police could have made him tell what he did to Quincy."

"I'll say this again, Mrs. Coleman." Sara called upon her professionalism, never mind she was sweating lightly and wearing running shorts and a tank top. "Michael isn't involved in your husband's disappearance."

"I see he has you completely fooled," she said, her eyes as hard as her husband's had been, using the same words he had, "just like he fooled my daughter."

Sara doubted she could say anything to change what Mrs. Coleman believed, but made a stab at it. "I'm sorry about what happened to your daughter, and I'm sorry your husband is missing, but I can't let you talk that way about Michael."

"Then maybe you'll listen to what my daughter has to say." Mrs. Coleman untied the ribbon from the packet of envelopes and pulled worn, white sheets of paper from the first two. Sara couldn't tell whether the slight breeze was rustling the paper or if her hands were shaking. "These are some of her letters."

"Mrs. Coleman, I hardly think this is necessary," Sara said.

"Well, I do," she snapped. "You need to understand what kind of man you're defending."

Mrs. Coleman began to read, her voice quivering.

I cry all the time. I'd do anything for him, but it's never enough.

He comes home late and gets angry when I ask where he's been. He's cheating on me. I just know it.

I think about coming back home, but I'd die without him. I never thought love would hurt like this.

Mrs. Coleman wiped away the trail of tears dripping down her face before looking up. "I could go on, but I've made my point."

Sara crossed her arms over her chest, not sure how to get across to a still-grieving mother that she didn't put much stock in what her daughter had written. Hadn't Laurie told her Chrissy had pursued Michael? If anything, Chrissy sounded as though she'd been obsessed with him. "And what point would that be?"

"That Michael Donahue can't be trusted! Can't you see that he's behind my husband's disappearance?"

Sara wondered if the woman knew Michael was one of the volunteers who'd joined in the search and that he was probably looking for her husband as they spoke. "You're wrong."

"Weren't you listening?" Mrs. Coleman cried. "Didn't what Chrissy wrote tell you anything?"

"It told me she was a very unhappy girl."

"Because of Donahue! My daughter is dead because of him. My husband could be dead, too. Because of him! And you took his case. You're helping him!"

"Like I already told you, I'm not his lawyer," Sara said, reining in her anger, reminding herself that the other woman was distraught because her husband was missing. "But I don't believe he's guilty of anything."

"You're sleeping with him, aren't you?" Mrs. Coleman accused. "That's why you won't believe me."

"It's none of your business who I'm sleeping with." Sara lifted her chin. Her car was parked in the lot just beyond the track. She didn't have to listen to this. "I'm going now."

She walked away, leaving Mrs. Coleman standing on the spongy surface of the track.

"You're a stupid, stupid girl." Mrs. Coleman called after her, waving one of the letters. Sara kept walking, but she couldn't get far enough away to avoid hearing the woman's parting shot. "Donahue's using you, just like he used Chrissy. By the time you realize that, it'll be too late."

CHAPTER TWELVE

THE CELL PHONE Laurie had tossed on the empty passenger seat rang, playing the tune of a love song she'd stupidly downloaded after her passionate night with Kenny.

She picked up the phone, verified from the on-screen prompt that it was indeed Kenny calling and shut it off.

She not only refused to talk to Kenny, she wasn't going to listen to the strains of "I Will Always Love You" even one more time. Too bad wiping the song from the phone's memory wouldn't bring an end to Kenny's renewed campaign to win her over.

He'd left her alone for exactly two days and two nights before he'd started in again last night with the phone calls. Here he was calling again at not quite nine in the morning.

If she didn't pick up at least once, he'd follow up with a personal visit. Before he did, she needed to shore up her defenses so that they were impenetrable.

She was getting there. Discovering Kenny had lied to get Chrissy Coleman's old boyfriend in trouble was definitely not a point in his favor.

The needle on her gas gauge pointed to empty. She made a quick turn into the station on her right and pulled in front of one of the pumps. Attached to the gas station was a popular repair shop the locals in Indigo Springs swore by.

She popped open the panel door over her fuel tank, twisted off the gas cap, yanked the nozzle off the pump and shoved it into the hole.

It rankled that even the mechanics going about their business made her think of Kenny.

Up until he was fired, he'd been one of them.

"Hey, Laurie." Will Turner, the grizzled, gray-haired owner of the shop, waved at her from across an expanse of pavement before disappearing into the back of the shop.

She took off after him, barely sparing a glance at the pump—it would shut off automatically.

She hurried past a car being hoisted by a hydraulic lift and a man in overalls bent over an engine before she spotted Will peering under the hood of an old Chevy. She called his name and he looked up.

"This area's off-limits to customers," Will said. "What are you doing back here, Laurie?"

She was chasing yet another reason to keep from going back to her ex-husband. "I need to know why you fired Kenny."

He frowned, moving away from the Chevy. He put a hand on her arm, steering her to a relatively quiet corner of the shop.

"I don't know where you got the idea I fired him. Kenny quit."

"Quit?" That didn't compute. "Why would he do that?"

"Darned if I know. That boy's the best mechanic I ever had. A born teacher, too. He's got a real knack for dealing with the young guys. I was hoping he'd take over the business when I retire."

"But Kenny drives you crazy." Back when she and Kenny were married, Kenny regularly overslept and got to work late or knocked off early without permission to hang out with his friends. "You fire him all the time."

"Haven't fired him more than once or twice in the last five years," Will said. The lines bracketing his eyes and mouth made Laurie realize he had to be in his sixties, at least. "Even then, I always hire him back. Be crazy not to."

"Then why haven't you hired him back this time?"

"Hardheaded bastard hasn't asked for his job back yet. Say, maybe you can get him to come on by. Maybe you can even get him to think about buying me out."

"You really think he's the right man to take over your business?"

"Hell, yeah. Too bad he doesn't think so." Will shook his head. "That Kenny, he never has thought enough of himself."

"That doesn't sound like the Kenny I know."

Will considered her for a moment. "Then maybe you don't know him as well as you think you do."

MICHAEL HUNG BACK on the fringes of the crowd of people milling about the outdoor community amphitheater Tuesday night, enjoying the laid-back atmosphere. Couples and young families, some with picnic baskets, spread blankets on the grass. A few senior citizens, a heavily pregnant woman and a girl on crutches claimed the limited bench seating in front of the stage.

"Not too shabby, huh?" Johnny crossed his arms over a chest that was swelling with pride.

"Yeah," Michael said, "put on a free concert and the crowds will come."

"Not the music," Johnny protested, his eyes comically wide. "The amphitheater."

"Oh, did you build that?"

"Sure did." Johnny's eyes suddenly narrowed. "You already know Pollock Construction built the amphitheater, don't you?"

Michael tried not to smile. "Your dad might have mentioned it."

Johnny's lips pursed. "Are you enjoying yourself?"

Michael couldn't hide his grin any longer. "As a matter of fact, I am."

"Go ahead. Have your fun. But wait till you hear the acoustics. See those laminated curved wood beams on the roof? They're the reason that amphitheater is a good little piece of work."

"If you do say so yourself," Michael said with a laugh.

"I wouldn't have to say so if you would," Johnny shot back good-naturedly. He inclined his head toward where Penelope sat on a blanket, beckoning to him. "Gotta go. The music's about to start. What are you doing here anyway?"

"Meeting Sara." Even the sound of her name brought him pleasure. "She thinks I should be seen out in public."

"Like that's gonna happen with you lurking

over here by these trees. When Sara gets here, come join us."

"Thanks," Michael said, liking the sound of the idea.

Something strange had happened since Sara suggested he become more visible in town—he'd begun to enjoy himself. She was largely responsible, of course, but Indigo Springs no longer seemed as objectionable.

The band broke into its opening number, a lively bluegrass tune. A few kids, no more than seven or eight years old, jumped to their feet and started to dance. Others joined in until a mass of children were clapping their small hands and stamping their little feet in a whirling, joyful circle.

"That's about the cutest thing I've ever seen." Laurie Grieb was suddenly standing next to him, the music having drowned out her approach, speaking to him as though they were already in the midst of a conversation. "It makes you want to get out there and dance with them."

"Yeah, it does," he agreed, surprised to discover it was true. One of the children spun around in tight little circles until he fell over like a top that had run out of steam. Laurie laughed. He'd always liked her despite her interest in Kenny, who'd never deserved her.

"Sara should be along soon." Before he could ask how she knew he was waiting for Sara, Laurie explained, "I overheard her on the phone this afternoon making plans to meet you. She's probably regrouping after the bad day she had."

That was the first he'd heard of Sara's bad day.

"The women's club canceling on her wouldn't have hit her so hard if she hadn't had that unpleasant visit from Jill Coleman this morning." Laurie kept on as though Sara had already filled him in on the day's events. "I understand Jill's upset about her husband, but really!"

He got a sick feeling in his stomach that he was the direct cause of Jill Coleman's visit. Apparently unaware of how strongly her comments had affected him, Laurie scanned the crowd. "You haven't seen Kenny, have you?"

"No," he said, his mind still on Sara.

"Let me ask you something. Did Kenny ever seem…um…unsure of himself to you?" Laurie's gaze fastened on him as though his answer mattered.

He tried to switch gears and focus on her question, but wasn't sure he'd understood. "Unsure of himself? Kenny?"

"Never mind." Laurie shook her head. "I shouldn't have asked that of you of all people. Kenny probably only seems like a jerk to you."

She had that right.

A woman who looked like an older version of Laurie, complete with frizzy hair, gestured wildly to her from the other side of the park.

"There's my mom," Laurie said. "Born and raised right here in PA and she loves bluegrass. Go figure."

Laurie left him with a little wave, picking her way through the crowd of people toward her mother's side. The band launched into another song as energetic as the first, and more people got up to dance.

Michael had been watching the park entrance for Sara, so he spotted her before she saw him. For long moments, he just stared. In low-rise tan slacks, chunky sandals and a form-fitting white shirt, with her brown hair long and loose, she looked like she belonged here in the park among the concert-goers. Like she belonged in Indigo Springs.

He'd do anything in his power, he realized, not to jeopardize that for her.

She smiled when she spotted him. Pleasure spiraled through him, the frustration he'd felt searching for a man nobody could find dissipating. She met him halfway, anchored her hands on his shoulders and kissed him briefly but sweetly on the lips.

"Hi," she said, smiling into his eyes. She smelled wonderful, like the peach-scented moisturizer she kept on a shelf in her bathroom and the warm scent that was uniquely hers.

"Hi, yourself."

The musicians on stage were the focal point of the evening but Michael noticed that some people in the crowd, probably all who knew he was a suspect in Quincy Coleman's disappearance, had witnessed the kiss.

He stepped back.

"Want to find a place to sit?" she asked close enough so he could hear, her warm breath teasing his ear.

He'd planned to lead her to the blanket where Johnny and Penelope sat listening to the music, saving a place for them. But that was before he'd talked to Laurie.

"I'd rather hear about your bad day," he said. "I ran into Laurie, and she said something about a women's club canceling on you."

"It's nothing." She waved off his concern.

"Why did they cancel?" he pressed, even as a likely reason occurred to him. "Is Jill Coleman a member of the club?"

"It doesn't matter if she is," she said. "I told you, it's not important."

Yet Michael feared it was vital.

"Let's get out of here," he said.

He thought she might protest, but after a moment's pause she nodded her agreement. They walked away from the park and the happy, laughing, dancing crowd, leaving the lively beat of the bluegrass music behind them.

Sara seemed content to walk in silence, perhaps sensing they'd reached a pivotal place in their relationship.

He wished they could keep walking straight out of town, that he didn't feel compelled to get the answers that would change everything.

"I hear Jill Coleman came to see you this morning," he said, breaking the silence. "Was it about me?"

They'd reached the quaint stone church where Penelope and Johnny had been married, which somehow seemed appropriate. He'd gotten his first glimpse of Sara inside this very church.

She didn't answer immediately, instead sitting down on the steps of the church. He joined her, resting his elbows on his knees, waiting her out.

"She had this misconception I was your lawyer," she said. "She was talking nonsense, trying to convince me to stop representing you."

"What did she say?" he prodded.

Based on set of her shoulders and the depth of her sigh, she didn't want to tell him. "She read me parts of some letters her daughter wrote her."

He must have gone pale because she put a hand on his arm. "I'm sure she took them out of context. Even if she didn't, the only thing they prove is that Chrissy was unhappy."

"What did she say the letters proved?"

Sara shook her head. "It doesn't matter."

"Then tell me."

She clamped her lips together, as though reluctant to let any words escape, but then finally she started to talk. "She said you were responsible for her husband's disappearance. Even if you weren't, you were using me and I shouldn't let you fool me the way you fooled Chrissy."

He was silent, digesting that. He'd tried to convince himself he wasn't hurting Sara's chances of integrating into the town, but it had become abundantly clear over the past few days that wasn't true.

Already Joe Wojokowski knew they were sleeping together. Jill Coleman had obviously figured it out, too. So far the damage to Sara had been minimal, but Michael foresaw trouble ahead. This time it had been a woman's club canceling her speaking engagement. Next time it might be an acquaintance who decided not to be a friend. Or a client who refused to walk through her door.

Her eyes seemed to ask him to contradict Jill Coleman's claims, but if he told Sara how deeply he was falling for her, she'd stick loyally by his side until he left town.

Then she'd be left with nothing.

"I hope you told that old busybody you were using me, too," he said. "I'd have liked to see her face when she found out our relationship was just about sex."

She stared at him, a bemused expression on her face. "I hadn't realized it was."

He forced himself to look her in the eyes, keeping everything he felt for her from his face. "Come on, Sara. You said you were fine with a short-term affair. We've known each other for less than two weeks. What else would it be about?"

"Mutual respect," she said, the bewilderment changing to hurt. "Caring."

"I care about you just fine," he said, "especially when we're in bed."

He could see her wondering why he was saying such hurtful things, but he couldn't give her the chance to cross examine him. He couldn't afford to have his facade crumble so he said the one thing guaranteed to put an end to whatever was growing between them.

"You're an even better lay than Chrissy was."

The moisture he'd seen gathering in her eyes dried up, and her expression hardened. She got up from the porch steps with the dignity of a queen.

"Let me walk you home," he said.

"Don't bother," she said coolly. "It seems like I'm going to take Mrs. Coleman's advice after all."

She strode away with her head held high and her shoulders thrown back, a woman who'd taken a blow and weathered it. His admiration for her grew, and he had to clutch the church railing to keep himself from rushing after her and taking everything back. He'd done the right thing, he told himself.

So why did the right thing hurt so much?

THE WHISTLE came from the open door of a storefront across the street, where construction workers were tearing up wooden floorboards with a pry bar.

Sara stopped and pivoted, her internal temperature rising. She wasn't going to take being whistled at. Not in her new hometown. Not this morning when she was officially open for business and when she was in a lousy mood.

Not after finding out Michael's interest in her was only sexual.

She marched across the street, mentally preparing her verbal attack, ready to blast whoever had whistled.

"Hi, Sara." Johnny Pollock exited the store, wearing one of his friendly smiles. "Hope you didn't mind the whistle. You didn't hear me when I yelled."

She joined him on the sidewalk, desperately trying to regain her poise, silently chastising herself for mistaking an innocent attempt to get her attention for a wolf call.

"Not at all," she lied, then gestured behind him to where one of his coworkers continued to rip out a portion of the wooden floor. "It looks like you're renovating."

"Just started this morning," he said. "The new owner's turning it into a candy store. When I got a chance, I was gonna head over to your office, but then I saw you walking by."

"What's up?" she asked. *Please don't mention Michael.* After the hurtful things he had said last night, she wasn't in the mood to hear his best friend champion him.

"I heard what happened with the women's club," he said.

She relaxed but only slightly. She wasn't keen

about discussing being blacklisted by Jill Coleman, either. "I guess it's true what they say about gossip and small towns."

"Indigo Springs isn't so small anymore," he said. "I only know about it because my mom's a member. She says they'll ask you to speak again once things settle down."

"You mean once Quincy Coleman is found?"

Johnny inclined his head. "Yeah. Mrs. Coleman's dead wrong to blame Michael, but it's bad timing to have his lawyer speak to the group."

Sara gritted her teeth, finding it ironic that she also had to speak Michael's name. "As I've already told Mrs. Coleman, I'm not Michael's lawyer."

"Okay. His girlfriend, then."

"I'm not his girlfriend, either." She'd been trying to convince herself that Michael had done her a favor last night. She'd been preparing to let him go anyway. Finding out he cared more about what they did in bed than about her should have made the whole process easier, but it hadn't.

Johnny looked surprised. "When did this happen?"

"Last night." She didn't give him a chance to comment. "Look, I've got to get going. I'm headed to Jimmy's Diner for coffee, then I need to get back to work."

"I could use some coffee, too. Did you know that you can get some at Abe's?" The general store was next door to the shop he was renovating. "Let me buy you a cup."

She hesitated, unwilling to get pulled into a conversation about Michael, but he seemed to have accepted that. "Sure."

Abe's General Store sold groceries and necessities like toiletries and first-aid supplies, just as Sara had expected. She didn't anticipate the nostalgic snack counter at the back of the store, with a line of five stools covered in red vinyl and an old-fashioned soda machine as a centerpiece.

"I had no idea this was back here," she told Johnny after he'd paid for their coffees and the girl behind the counter left to help in another part of the store. Sara had intended to take her coffee and go, but the atmosphere made her want to linger. "That soda machine looks like an antique."

"It's worth quite a bit," he said. "That's why Michael got time in juvenile detention."

Sara felt as though she'd been blindsided. "Excuse me?"

"Did he tell you he got arrested for breaking and entering when we were high-school seniors?"

"Yes, he did," she said, cursing herself for

agreeing to have coffee with him, "but I don't want to—"

"Did he tell you I was with him?" Johnny interrupted. He rubbed the back of his neck. "No, he wouldn't have. He never told anybody, even though it was my idea. And all because of a damn cherry cola."

He wasn't making sense, but neither had Michael's bare-bones version of the story.

"Abe wouldn't serve him," Johnny continued. "He died a couple of years ago, but he used to be tight with Quincy Coleman. He told Michael not to come around anymore."

Sara wasn't a good enough actress to pretend she wasn't interested in his story. "Because Michael was dating Chrissy?"

"He wasn't dating her exactly, but she was always coming around, making it clear she was hot for him." Johnny inhaled, his eyes trained on the stainless-steel soda machine instead of on her. "The lock on the back door was pretty flimsy. Michael followed me into the store, trying to get me to leave, but I wanted to pour him that damn cherry cola. When we heard the sirens, it was too late."

"I didn't know you got arrested, too."

"That's just it. I didn't. Michael said I'd lose my spot on the wrestling team and my college scholarship if they caught me." He paused, tapping the countertop. "So I hid behind this very counter and let him take the fall."

"How could you?" Sara cried.

"I'm not proud of it," he said. "My dad's the only other person who knows what I did. By the time I told him, though, Michael was already in juvenile detention. Nothing I said would change that, so I kept quiet."

Sara thought about the strength of character it had taken a teenage boy to sacrifice himself for his friend. "Now I understand why you and your dad feel the way you do about Michael."

"That's not the only reason." Johnny had been staring straight ahead while he told his story, but now he looked at her. "You've gotten to know Michael. You know what kind of person he is."

She swallowed the lump of emotion in her throat because she didn't know anything after last night. "Why are you telling me this?"

"Because Michael's got a protective streak as wide as the Lehigh. I'm assuming he found out about the women's club last night. If he was the one who broke things off with you, it might not be because he doesn't care about you." Johnny paused, giving his next words more weight. "It could be because he cares too much."

THE LAST PLACE Sara expected to find herself later that afternoon was in front of Felicia Feldman's house.

She had no intention of seeking out Michael despite what Johnny had told her. As a lawyer, Sara dealt in facts. Johnny's claim that Michael cared about her was purely conjecture.

If Sara hadn't known Mrs. Feldman planned to spend the day gardening, she wouldn't be here. But the woman was so anxious for news on Sara's efforts to get her loan refinanced that she'd left word where she'd be at all times.

Sara didn't only have news. She had big news. The kind of information that should be delivered in person, even if she ran the risk of running into Michael.

Mrs. Feldman was bent over a colorful flower bed beside the house she was so desperate not to lose, a floppy hat shielding her face from the sun. She dug in the soil with a trowel, a small pile of weeds next to her.

"Hi, Mrs. Feldman," Sara said, announcing her presence. Mrs. Feldman looked up, the hope on her face visible.

"I've got some great news," she told the woman without preamble. "I found a lender who's agreed to refinance your loan."

Mrs. Feldman grew perfectly still, with only

her mouth moving as she asked in a cautious voice, "Does that mean I can keep my house?"

"That's exactly what it means."

Mrs. Feldman let out a joyful cry, dropped the small trowel, scrambled to her feet and wrapped Sara in a hug. She smelled of the sun, the earth and happiness.

"Oh, thank you, thank you!" Her hug was surprisingly robust considering her small stature. "You're a miracle worker!"

Sara laughed. "I wouldn't go that far."

"You are." Mrs. Feldman finally let her go, her bemusement temporarily surpassing her joy. "I thought nobody would give me a loan because of my credit history."

"That's what I thought, too, but this particular lender offers a special program for people like you." Sara didn't tell her about the long odds the loan officer had quoted when she first contacted him. "The interest rate is higher than I would have liked, but the payments are manageable if you stick to a budget."

"Oh, I will. I'd never risk losing my home again." She smiled. "I wish Michael was here so I could tell him!"

Relief that she wouldn't have to face Michael mixed with concern over his whereabouts. "Where is he?" she asked, hoping she sounded casual, hoping Michael wasn't out searching for Quincy Coleman again.

"I'm not sure," Mrs. Feldman said. "He said something about picking up a new part for my downstairs toilet. He's always doing something for me. This morning he replaced two of my ceiling fans."

"I'm glad you two are getting along."

"Did he tell you that?" Mrs. Feldman asked anxiously.

"Well, no," Sara admitted. "From what you said, I just assumed things are better between you."

"They're not. He's hardly here, and we don't talk to each other when he is. He'll never forgive me for what I did."

Sara chastised herself for getting pulled into yet another discussion about Michael, but Mrs. Feldman appeared so distressed she could hardly backtrack now. "Have you told him you're sorry?"

"I tried to, just like you suggested, but he told me to forget it. That it was all in the past." She chewed on her lower lip before continuing. "If it was really in the past, things would be better between us."

"Then tell him you love him," Sara said, the

solution appearing obvious now that she'd proposed it. "Your love is what he thought he lost when your husband threw him out. That's what he needs to know he still has."

Mrs. Feldman's eyes grew wide. "I think you're right."

"Then tell him," Sara urged, eager to help mend the rift between great-aunt and nephew. She wasn't as keen on examining why it was important that Michael know somebody loved him.

Mrs. Feldman captured her wrist, a wealth of feeling in her expression. "I'm so glad you and Michael found each other. I can tell how much in love you are."

Sara felt a thickness in her throat, but managed to reply, "You're wrong. We're not in love."

"That can't be true!" Mrs. Feldman seemed genuinely shocked. "I've seen the way you look at each other."

"It is true," Sara said, even as it registered that Mrs. Feldman was the second person that day who refused to believe Michael didn't care about her.

Now that Sara was getting over the shock and the hurt, she wondered why she'd so easily accepted Michael's claim that their relationship was about sex. If that were true, wouldn't he have slept with her the first night they met? Had she been caught so unawares that she hadn't thought his explanation all the way through?

A police cruiser pulled over to the curb in front of Mrs. Feldman's house, effectively ending her introspection. The two front doors opened simultaneously, and Chief Jackson and Officer Wojokowski got out of the car. They walked to the flower bed, the chief a head taller than his officer, their heavy steps trampling the grass, their faces solemn.

"Afternoon, ladies," Chief Jackson said in his courtly style. Wojokowski was silent, his eyes scanning the yard. "Is Michael home?"

Something wasn't right, Sara thought, trying to figure it out while Mrs. Feldman repeated the same story she'd told Sara about Michael's whereabouts.

Chief Jackson nodded to the PT Cruiser parked in front of his squad car. "That is Michael Donahue's rental car, right?"

Sara stepped in front of Mrs. Feldman, not liking the direction of the chief's questions. "Can I ask what this is about?"

He produced a piece of paper she instantly recognized. "I have a warrant to search his car."

"On what grounds?" Sara challenged even as she took the warrant from him and began scanning the contents.

"On the grounds that the car might contain evidence connected to Quincy Coleman's disappearance."

The document was in order. Legally speaking, Sara could do nothing to stop the police from searching Michael's car. After advising Mrs. Feldman to stay where she was, Sara trailed the officers to the PT Cruiser. Michael had made it easy for them by leaving the car unlocked. Sara watched with growing unease as the two policemen combed the interior before popping open the trunk.

Chief Jackson reached the back of the car first, bending over to get a better look inside the trunk. He straightened almost immediately, his face grim. "Wojo, bring an evidence bag over here."

"Got one, Chief." Wojo, who was already headed in the police chief's direction, didn't break his stride.

"What? What did you find?" Sara asked as Wojo reached into the trunk with a gloved hand and pulled out what looked to be the kind of small towel that attached to a golf bag. He held it up, revealing that it was streaked with blood.

"That towel doesn't prove a thing if it's not Mr. Coleman's blood," Sara said, her heart racing even as she issued the defense.

Wojo flipped the towel around so she could get a better look. Two initials were monogrammed onto the cloth: *QC*.

"On the contrary, Ms. Brenneman," Chief Jackson said, "this should be enough to get a warrant for Michael Donahue's arrest."

CHAPTER THIRTEEN

SARA'S MIND rebelled at the implications of a bloody towel being found in Michael's rental car.

She simply did not believe that the hero at the river, the man who'd stuck around to help the aunt who betrayed him, had hurt Quincy Coleman.

There had to be another explanation.

"The car wasn't locked," she pointed out. "It's been parked on the street all night. Anybody could have popped the trunk and planted that evidence."

"In the movies, maybe," Chief Jackson countered, "but this is real life."

"The warrant says you were tipped off to search the car, but it doesn't say by who. Why not?"

"I'm not at liberty to say."

Sara didn't believe that. Her guess was that an anonymous tipster had phoned in the information. In that case, a judge shouldn't have granted the warrant. Even though Sara wasn't a criminal lawyer, she knew judges could be talked into awarding trusted law-enforcement personnel special favors—especially when they claimed to be closing in on a guilty party.

"Things would go easier for Donahue if he turned himself in," Chief Jackson said. If he'd ever believed Quincy Coleman had disappeared of his own volition, he clearly no longer did. "If either you or Mrs. Feldman know where he is, you give him that message."

Chief Jackson tipped his hat, then sauntered to his patrol car to join Wojokowski, as though the matter of Michael's guilt was already settled. Mrs. Feldman hurried to Sara's side, asking to be filled in on what had happened.

"What are we going to do?" she asked when Sara was through briefing her, her face once again lined with worry, her relief over being able to keep her house gone.

"Exactly what the chief told us to do," Sara decided. "We'll contact Michael and tell him to turn himself in."

"We can't do that! Chief Jackson thinks Michael killed Quincy."

"And we know he didn't," Sara said. "Michael's the only one who can clear this up. I'll get my cell phone and give him a call."

She hurried to her car to retrieve her purse,

thankful she'd programmed Michael's number into her phone, but the device wasn't where she usually kept it.

She tried to remember when she'd last used the phone. It had been this morning; her mother had called and, hearing her voice, had instantly guessed something was wrong. After assuring her the move to Indigo Springs wasn't a mistake, Sara hung up, marveled that her mom hadn't figured out that her daughter's heart was breaking—and left the phone lying on her desk.

Sara didn't waste time. Within moments she was on the landline in Mrs. Feldman's kitchen, explaining to Laurie why she needed Michael's number.

"This is wild," Laurie said. "It sounds like somebody's trying to frame Mike."

"That's the only thing that makes sense," Sara agreed.

"Who do you think it is?" Laurie made a sound of disgust. "Don't answer that. We both know it's Kenny."

Sara had grown accustomed to Laurie's bluntness, but her office manager's declaration surprised her. A fool could tell Laurie was still in love with her ex-husband. "The possibility crossed my mind," she said carefully.

"It's more than a possibility!" Laurie exclaimed, and Sara could almost feel fumes shooting through the phone line. "Kenny's been rotten to Mike since he came back to town. Heck, he's always been rotten to Mike. Who else—"

"Laurie, stop," Sara interrupted before the other woman could get on one of her verbal rolls. "We can talk about this later. Right now I really need that number."

Sara called Michael seconds after she disconnected with the still angry Laurie. The phone rang twice before the line filled with an inexplicable silence. Sara waited a few seconds before disconnecting, facing her initial fear that Michael was in the woods searching for Coleman, out of cell-phone range.

The logical next step was calling Pollock Construction to find out if either Johnny or his father knew where Michael was. She intended to call information for the number of the business but hit redial at the last second.

"Sara?" Michael picked up on the first ring, his voice surprisingly clear and strong. And worried. "Is something wrong? Are you okay?"

"I'm fine," she said.

"Is it Aunt Felicia?" He sounded concerned, the way only a decent man could sound—a decent man Sara very much feared was being framed for a crime he wasn't capable of committing.

"Your aunt's fine, too," she reassured him.

She'd meant to tell him to meet her at the police station, but once the police started questioning Michael, they'd be less likely to follow up on clues that could lead them to discover what really happened to Quincy Coleman.

"How far are you from Coleman's house?" she asked.

"Maybe a fifteen-minute walk."

"I need you to go directly there," she ordered. "Don't talk to anybody if you can help it. Just get there."

"Why?"

She debated only briefly with herself before justifying her response. "I have a new piece of evidence to show you."

With luck, it might even turn out to be true.

CHASING DOWN that no good ex-husband of hers was becoming a habit Laurie needed to break.

And she would, just as soon as she marched him into the Indigo Springs Police Department and forced him to tell Chief Jackson he'd planted false evidence in Mike Donahue's trunk.

But first she had to wake him up. Even though she was looking for him, it ticked her off. It was eleven freaking o'clock. He should be up and around, contributing to society.

Logically she knew she shouldn't be inside her old house, her beloved dog at her heels, only steps away from the bed she used to share with Kenny. The bed in which she'd made love with him only two nights ago. She hadn't even tried to resist twisting the doorknob when her knock went unanswered and she heard Valentine's barks. The yearning to say a quick hello to the dog was too great to ignore. Besides, if Kenny didn't want intruders, he could have engaged the lock.

She marched to the bedroom windows and pulled up the shades, letting sun stream into the room and over the sleeping Kenny. He flung an arm over his eyes.

"Get up, Kenny," she said harshly.

The arm dropped and he bolted to a sitting position, exposing his bare hair-sprinkled chest. His head jerked to where she stood by the window and he instantly relaxed, his face curving into a smile.

"Well, hi there, Laurie." The smile grew. "I was hoping to get you back in my bedroom."

She braced herself against him, which was harder than it might have been if stubble hadn't covered his lower face and his hair wasn't messy. The jerk always had looked sexiest in the morning.

"I'm not staying," she retorted. "And neither

are you. Get dressed so you can tell Chief Jackson how you're trying to frame Michael Donahue."

"What?" He swung a leg that was as bare as the rest of him out of bed. "I don't know what—"

"I'm not having this conversation with a naked man." Laurie turned away before he got out of bed. Kenny had put on a few pounds since they'd been married but he still looked damn fine. "I'll be in the living room when you're decent."

She slammed the bedroom door shut, then paced to the living room, Valentine at her heels. The room was the same as she remembered, down to the casual overstuffed furniture they'd gotten secondhand from her parents and the Van Gogh and Monet prints she'd hung on the wall. The only difference was a metal desk in the corner with a computer on top.

She inadvertently bumped the desk, turning off the screen saver on the oversized monitor. The computer flashed on.

"Congratulations!" the screen read. "You have passed Unix Level One!"

She moved closer. At the bottom of the screen was the name of a technical university.

The bedroom door opened and Kenny emerged, pulling an Indigo River Rafters T-shirt over his head. He was wearing shorts and his feet were bare.

"Are you taking an online course?" she asked before he could say anything.

His eyes went to the computer, and he blew out a breath. "Yeah, I am. I was up half the night trying to pass that damn Unix test."

"I don't understand. That sounds like computer programming. Are you switching careers?"

He rubbed a hand over his face. "Trying to. If I can get through the curriculum."

"I thought you liked being a mechanic."

"I did," he said. "I do."

"Then why quit your job?"

"Because of you, okay?" He sat down on the sofa and rested his head in his hands. "I thought you'd be more likely to come back to me if I had an impressive job."

"What does your job have to do with it?"

He let out a harsh laugh. "Are you kidding? Like you really would have married a mechanic if you hadn't been pregnant."

"What's wrong with being a mechanic? Especially when you're the best one around." Laurie stopped, the rest of what he'd said belatedly registering. "And what do you mean I wouldn't have married you if I wasn't pregnant? I married you because I loved you."

His head jerked up, as though he wasn't sure he believed her. "Then why did you leave me?"

She could say it was because at nineteen he'd been too irresponsible to be a husband, but she was tired of skirting the truth. "Because I was never going to mean as much to you as Chrissy."

"What? That's not true!"

"I'm not stupid, Kenny. I know you never got over her, that she's the reason you still hate Mike Donahue."

He was shaking his head. She'd made the mistake of getting too near him. He captured her hand, pulling her down on the sofa beside him. He took both her hands in his. She should pull away, but the grave look on his face made her stay put.

"I feel terrible about what happened to Chrissy, but I was never in love with her," he said. "Sure, I liked that a popular girl like her paid attention to me, but it didn't break my heart when she dumped me."

He looked earnest, but Laurie was afraid to believe him. "Then why do you hate Mike so much? Why did you put that bloody towel in his trunk?"

"Whoa! What bloody towel?"

He shook his head throughout her entire explanation of what the police had found in Michael's PT Cruiser. "I'd never do anything like that."

"Then why did you lie to the cops about hearing him threaten to kill Mr. Coleman?" she retorted.

"Okay, you got me," he said. "That was wrong. But Donahue will come through okay. A guy like him always does."

"What do you mean, a guy like him?"

"Oh, come on, Laurie. When we were in high school, other kids looked up to him even *after* he got out of juvenile detention. Johnny Pollock was always talking him up, telling people what a great friend he was. You thought he was cool, too. You still do, with his Peace Corps job and that selfless act of his."

"You're jealous," Laurie accused, instinctively knowing she was right.

"So what if I am?"

"There's no reason for you to be jealous. You know my boss has a thing for Mike, right?"

"What's to stop you from having a thing for him, too?"

She took a breath, then a leap of faith. "You, Kenny. I've only ever had a thing for you."

A look of awe came over his face and he reached for her, but she put a hand on his chest.

"Before we try this again, we need to get a couple of things straight. One, you have to tell the police Mike didn't threaten to kill Mr. Coleman."

"I will," he said.

She kept her hand planted on his chest. "And two, you need to drop that computer course and ask Will Turner for your job back. If you take classes, they should be business classes so you can own your own garage one day. You need to start believing in yourself the way I believe in you."

He smiled at her. Valentine jumped up and down on the carpet at their feet, clamoring for attention.

"What are you thinking?" she asked.

"I'm thinking that even though you talk way too much, I'm never gonna stop loving you."

She smiled back, going willingly as he gathered her more fully into his arms. There was nothing she could add that would make this moment—this *reunion*—more perfect.

MICHAEL REACHED the edge of the woods behind Quincy Coleman's house and stopped as if he'd slammed into a brick wall, riveted by the sight of Sara peering through a window on the rear porch.

She stood back, her hands on her hips in what appeared to be frustration. She should have looked polished and professional in flats, wide-legged slacks and an unstructured jacket with three-quarter-length sleeves, but the aura of being in control she usually projected was gone.

When he'd gotten her call about the new piece of evidence, he was within easy walking distance of Coleman's house because he'd remembered a cave he'd stumbled across as a teenager. He found bat droppings inside instead of Quincy Coleman.

The promise of a new clue had brought him to Coleman's house, his hope rekindled that the missing man would soon be found. But standing here, watching Sara, he realized the prospect of seeing her had been just as much a draw as his hope.

He emerged from the cover of the trees, expecting Sara to wait for him to reach the porch, but she hurried down the steps, rushing across the lawn. The sun bathed her face, highlighting the faint worry lines that creased her brow.

He fought not to reach for her and assure her that whatever was troubling her would be okay. He'd forfeited the right to touch her when he'd lied and said he only cared about her in relation to sex.

"Has anyone seen you since I called?" she asked, not bothering with a greeting, a not-so-subtle by-product of the cavalier way he'd treated her.

"No," he said. The professional search teams had moved on to more distant sections of the woods, and most of the volunteers had returned to their day jobs. After nearly four days with no sign of the man, most people had given him up for dead. He'd heard that tomorrow the police planned to call in cadaver dogs. "Why?"

"Chief Jackson is looking for you. He's going to arrest you," she said.

He listened with disbelief and frustration to her account of the bloody towel being found in the trunk of his rental car.

"I'm going to the police station to clear this up," he declared when she was through.

"No!" She put a hand on his arm, the first time she'd touched him since he'd said those cruel things. Just as quickly, she took her hand away. "You can't go to the police yet. We don't know what else they have on you. It's pretty obvious someone's trying to frame you."

She hadn't asked for an explanation of how Coleman's monogrammed towel had ended up in his trunk. She'd given him the benefit of the doubt, as she had since the moment they met. He cleared his throat, trying to camouflage how much her blind faith in him meant to him. "So you think it's Coleman's blood on the towel?"

"I'd be surprised if it wasn't. But it didn't

look like a new towel, and there wasn't a lot of blood on it. Maybe Coleman was using it as a rag. Didn't you say Kenny Grieb's parents live next door? Maybe Coleman cut himself when he was working in the yard, and Kenny saw the towel lying around and grabbed it."

"That's a lot of maybes," Michael said.

"I know," she said. "Even if Kenny did plant that towel in your trunk, we can't prove it."

"Then let's focus on that new piece of evidence."

She grimaced. "Here's where I confess I haven't found it yet."

He didn't understand. "Excuse me?"

"I thought—okay, hoped—the police missed something, but it looks like somebody's already cleaned up in Coleman's kitchen. We can't get in the house without permission anyway."

Her comment drove home that, as a lawyer, she was duty bound to play by the rules. "You said Chief Jackson is looking for me. Aren't you required to bring me in?"

"We both know Coleman's probably dead," she said instead of answering his question. "If we don't figure out what really happened to him, you'll be charged with murder."

He didn't deserve her support, not after he'd deliberately pushed her away. "Why does it matter so much to you?" he asked, suddenly needing to know.

"It'd matter to me if any innocent man went to prison," she answered, which was what he deserved but not what he wanted to hear. Idiot that he was, he'd been hoping she still cared about him.

"Then let's see if the garage is unlocked," he suggested, hiding his disappointment.

"Good idea," she said.

He surveyed their surroundings as they walked together to the detached concrete structure, grateful not to see any lurking neighbors who might alert the police. Just in case, he wasted little time going directly to the side-entrance. The door was unlocked, as it had been the night Wojo had followed him.

"You sure you want to come in?" Michael asked, his hand still on the doorknob, worried about the possible repercussions she might face. "It could be bad news if we got caught."

"Then we won't get caught," she said. "So let's be quick about this."

Arguing with her would be useless so he preceded her into the garage, his impressions the same as they had been the afternoon he'd argued with Coleman. The interior of the building was just short of immaculate, the motorbike the only thing that seemed out of place.

"I've never seen such a neat garage." Sara's sigh was audible. "I don't know if we'll find any clues here."

"I thought the motorbike was a clue." Michael told her about leaving her bed to check if it was still in the garage and his theory that Coleman might have covered a lot of ground if he'd been on a motorbike instead of on foot. "But, as you can see, it's still here."

Sara walked over to the motorbike, running her fingers over the curved handlebars. "I wonder why Coleman has one. He seems pretty active, but I doubt many men his age ride them."

"Chrissy used to have a motorbike," Michael said. "It could be the same one. Maybe he couldn't bring himself to get rid of it."

"That makes sense." She gestured to a garishly painted ceramic ashtray on one of the counters that looked like the work of a third-grader. Above it, a faded painting of a stick-figure family hung from the wall. Beside the painting were a dozen or more unframed photos. "Look at these."

Only a few of the photos contained either of the elder Colemans. Most were of Chrissy, their only child. Michael focused on a close-up of the blond, blue-eyed girl he remembered. She was frozen in time, destined to grow no older than her teens.

"She was pretty," Sara said quietly. "What was she like?"

Willful. Headstrong. Manipulative.

The words jumped to mind, but he swallowed them. He wasn't about to malign a girl who would still be alive if not for him.

"She liked to have fun," he said. "And she liked to get her own way."

"Don't we all?" Sara said wistfully.

Sara moved slowly from left to right, with Michael looking over her shoulder, past photo after photo of Chrissy. Chrissy in a tutu. In a cheerleader's uniform. In a prom dress. In shorts and sunglasses. In a bathing suit.

His eyes swung back to the photo of Chrissy wearing the dark, oversized shades. It was one of the few that included Quincy Coleman. Father and daughter stood beside each other, wearing twin smiles.

Standing in front of identical motorbikes.

"Do you see that, Michael?" Sara gestured to the photo he was examining, excitement in her voice. "The Colemans have two motorbikes. You could have been on the right track the other night. Coleman could have gone into the woods on a bike."

"They *had* two motorbikes," he said slowly, his theory suddenly seeming full of holes. "Chances are Coleman got rid of one."

"But look at this garage. It's full of things that would remind him of Chrissy. Why dump the motorbike?"

"I only saw one the last time I was here."

"You weren't specifically looking for another one," she argued. "It could have been beneath a tarp. Or in the shed in the backyard."

"I don't know, Sara," he said slowly. "The more I think about it, the more far-fetched it seems. When Chrissy was alive, she and her dad used to go to an off-road track. They don't allow motorbikes on the mountain-bike paths around here."

"But didn't you say Coleman was upset? That he'd been drinking? What makes you think he'd follow the rules? Couldn't he have gone into the woods behind his house and picked up a trail?"

Michael had entertained that same scenario just a few nights ago. "That's a good point, but the bike trails around here are well-used. If Coleman had had an accident on one of the trails, somebody would have found him by now."

"Not if he took a wrong turn. It rained pretty heavily on Saturday. And heaven knows there's a lot of woods to search."

"Those paths are well-marked. It's hard to veer off one. They even put up signs when…" His voice trailed off as he remembered a warning he and Johnny had stumbled across when they were searching for Coleman. They'd been on the outer edge of the designated search area, farther than a man could have reached on foot. "I think I might know where to look."

DANGER: EROSION. Sara read the sign blocking off a section of a mountain-bike path that was a short hike from the spot on the shoulder of a two-lane, twisting road where Michael had directed Sara to park.

They'd spent the past ten minutes in silence while they walked under the canopy of trees, the beauty of the weekday afternoon surrounding them. With each step, Sara felt as though they were getting closer to solving the mystery of Quincy Coleman's disappearance.

She was no nearer to figuring out whether she bought Johnny Pollock's theory that Michael had pushed her away to protect her, and Mrs. Feldman's claim that Michael loved her.

She wanted to believe both statements, just as she longed to believe they'd find Quincy Coleman alive, but she was afraid all of those scenarios were long shots.

"The ground's still pretty soft." Michael broke the silence, toeing the beaten-down path with his hiking boot. "I don't see any tracks, but the rain might have washed them away."

He stepped over the chain stretched across the section of path, then held out a hand to Sara. She let him help her, pretending she didn't notice the electric moment when their hands touched.

They started along a section that was about six feet wide and level, but it quickly started ascending and soon narrowed to approximately half its width. Portions of the left side of the path had crumbled into the hillside.

"Stay as far to the right as you can." Michael made a barrier with his outstretched arm, wordlessly promising to catch her if she stumbled.

Protecting her.

"This path is narrow even for someone on foot." Sara prided herself on being in shape but she was slightly out of breath from the uphill climb. "If Coleman went this way, it seems he would have turned back."

"Yeah, it does." Michael sounded unaffected by the exertion, as though he was the runner instead of her. "Let's go to the top of that rise. If we don't see him, we'll turn back."

The increasingly difficult climb proved to be

worth the effort for aesthetic value alone. With the sun shining and the grass lush from the recent rain, the view from the crest to the valley below was postcard-perfect. The world looked green for as far as the eye could see, but Sara spotted neither motorbike nor man.

"It was worth a try," Sara said, "but there's nobody here except us."

"Well, we both knew it was a shot in the dark." Michael started descending the path, holding out a hand to help Sara navigate a slick spot. She took his hand at the same moment she heard something cry out. They both froze.

"Did you hear that?" she whispered.

"Shhh," he said, her hand still tucked in his. They stood perfectly still, only their breathing audible in the stillness of the afternoon.

"Help!" The cry was weak but unmistakably human.

"It's coming from down there." Michael indicated the hillside that dropped steeply from the path. He dropped her hand and ventured to the edge of the path, peering over the side.

"Oh, my God! It's Coleman," Michael said. "It looks like he's hurt."

"Give me your cell phone." Sara waited while Michael unhooked it from the clip on his waist, then grabbed it, all the while praying he had service. One bar showed up on the screen—not much but enough.

"Hang on, Mr. Coleman! Help is coming!" Michael shouted down the hillside. To Sara, he said, "Stay here. I'll go down and wait with him."

The dispatcher who answered the emergency call was a local, familiar with the road where Sara had parked. Sara quickly described the direction in which she and Michael had walked, and the dispatcher promised to send help.

After disconnecting, it occurred to Sara that one of them should meet the rescue team halfway. She scrambled down the hill, following the path Michael had taken, intending to volunteer to stay with Coleman if her rudimentary first-aid skills were better than his.

Quincy Coleman lay on a tiered section of hillside about twenty yards from the point where his motorbike had left the path. The bike lay in a mangled heap ten yards farther below. He was positioned awkwardly, with one leg under him and the other outstretched, leading Sara to guess he'd broken a limb.

Michael was crouched beside Coleman, his back to Sara, one of his large hands on Coleman's narrow shoulders. He held the water bottle he'd brought along to Coleman's parched lips, making sure the man took small sips so he wouldn't get sick.

"Just bear with me a little while longer," Michael said. "It looks like your leg's broken and you're probably suffering from exposure, but the EMTs will get you off this mountain and fix you right up."

"So sorry," Coleman croaked. Sara moved nearer, straining to hear him. "My fault."

"Lots of people have motorbike accidents," Michael said. "Nobody's blaming you."

"No, no." Coleman shook his head, obviously agitated. "Sorry about Chrissy. Sorry I blamed you. My fault. My fault."

He seemed on the edge of delirium. Michael must have realized that, too, because his voice gentled. "Take it easy. You don't know what you're saying."

"But I do." Coleman's voice was rusty from disuse but he kept talking, rasping out his sentences. "Lot of time to think. Told Chrissy… never wanted to see her again if she left with you. Never did."

It seemed to cost Coleman precious energy to talk. Once again Michael put the water bottle to his lips, offering the man small sips.

"You shouldn't blame yourself," Michael said. "You couldn't have known what would happen."

"Should have known. She was sad, so sad." Now that his throat had been lubricated, Coleman's voice sounded stronger. "She called me. Said she was unhappy and wanted to come home. I told her she wasn't welcome. A day later, she was dead."

Coleman's face, white with pain and partly covered with gray stubble, crumpled in misery. If he hadn't been dehydrated, Sara thought tears would be flowing freely down his cheeks.

"No, Mr. Coleman," Michael said firmly. "We both know Chrissy died because of me."

Coleman's head shook back and forth. "Not true. Used you as a scapegoat. Knew it all along."

"Knew what?" Michael asked.

Coleman's eyes closed, and Sara thought he might have passed out from the pain. She heard the rustling of leaves, the songs of birds, the whoosh of the wind. Then Coleman opened his eyes and said, "Knew you weren't driving the night she died."

Sara inhaled sharply, waiting for Michael to deny Coleman's claim. Long moments passed, and she realized he wasn't going to. He crouched there, the young man who'd been so grievously wronged beside the old man who'd wronged him, and said, "It doesn't matter now."

But Michael was wrong, Sara thought as she made her way back up the hill to meet the rescue team, having decided not to intrude on their private moment.

It mattered a great deal.

CHAPTER FOURTEEN

BY THE TIME night fell on Indigo Springs, the darkness didn't seem as black. It could have been due to the glow of the moon, which cast enough light for Michael to navigate the steps carved into the hillside, but it could also have been so many other things.

Quincy Coleman, bruised and battered on the mountaintop, apologizing for the hell he'd put Michael through after Chrissy's death.

So sorry. Used you as a scapegoat.

Chase Bradford shaking his hand after the emergency team lifted Coleman to level ground in a Stokes basket, apologizing for letting the trouble he'd been having with his girlfriend stop him from making the effort to get to know Michael.

Johnny kept telling me you were one of the good guys, and he was right.

Chief Jackson sidling up to Michael as he

took a shift helping carry Coleman's stretcher through the woods to a waiting ambulance.

I'm sorry, son. I was wrong about you.

Aunt Felicia, her eyes watering and her lips trembling, speaking words she'd never before said to him.

I love you, Michael.

And the night wasn't yet over.

He needed to set things right with Sara before it was. He hadn't seen her since they'd found Coleman. She hadn't stuck around when the rescue team arrived, an appointment she had scheduled with a potential client drawing her back to town.

He found her behind her house on the private deck that overlooked the woods, a glass of red wine in hand as she swayed gently on her new porch swing.

"Hi, Sara." He announced his arrival so he wouldn't startle her, but she didn't seem surprised to see him. "I called your phones but didn't get an answer. It finally dawned on me you'd be back here."

Her own little slice of heaven, she'd called it.

"A strange thing happened this afternoon," she said. "Some deliverymen showed up to install a porch swing. When I called the store to ask who sent it, they said you had."

He sat down beside her, understanding perhaps for the first time what had attracted her to the town. Tranquility, once you'd found it, would be hard to give up. Now that the mystery of what had happened to Quincy Coleman had been solved, life in Indigo Springs would return to normal. For Sara, the tranquility would return. He'd tried to help it along.

"I knew you wanted one," he said, "but I'll leave the mint juleps up to you."

They both knew he wouldn't be around to drink them.

"Thank you," she said.

"You're welcome," he said.

In the ensuing quiet, an owl hooted.

"Did you hear that Quincy Coleman's going to be all right?" Sara asked, breaking the silence.

"I heard." He'd wormed the information out of a nurse at the hospital where the EMTs had taken the injured man. Coleman was dehydrated and had a broken leg but he'd held up surprisingly well for a man his age.

"I talked to Laurie a little while ago. She said Kenny denies he planted that evidence in your trunk, but he's going to apologize for lying to the police. She says he wants to make peace with you."

Her remark dovetailed nicely into what he'd

come to tell her, but he had difficulty squeezing the words out of his suddenly dry throat. "That's not going to happen unless he catches up with me tonight. I'm leaving in the morning."

She drank the rest of her wine, setting the glass down on the small table next to the porch swing. Her face was angled away from him so he couldn't see her expression. "So you've decided to take that assignment in Ghana?"

"Yes," he said. "Once I let my recruiter know I'm on board, things will move pretty quickly."

And then, for the next two years of his life, he could concern himself with solving the problems of other people instead of his own.

"I assume your aunt told you she can keep her house," she said.

"She did. We're both grateful to you for that." He paused because that wasn't the most important thing his great-aunt had told him. "Aunt Felicia apologized for not standing up to her husband when he kicked me out."

Sara nodded once, giving away nothing.

"She said you were the one who encouraged her to say she was sorry," he added.

"I suggested she tell you what was in her heart," Sara said. "To get everything out in the open where it couldn't hurt either of you anymore."

"Thank you," he said. Considering she'd

given him back something invaluable—the love of family—the two simple words seemed inadequate.

"Speaking of getting things out in the open, I overheard Mr. Coleman talking to you on the mountain," she said. "I didn't mean to, but I did."

He'd been so caught up in Coleman's confession that it hadn't occurred to him that Sara was within earshot. He waited, wishing she'd drop the subject, knowing she wouldn't.

She turned and looked at him fully for the first time since he'd joined her on the porch swing. "Is it true you weren't driving the night Chrissy died?"

The question was simple but the answer more complicated than an algebraic equation. He'd bottled up the truth for so long that he wasn't sure he could set it free, but this was Sara. Sara, who'd never judged him.

"It's true." He stared into the darkness, but saw Chrissy at the wheel, crying hysterically, refusing to slow down. He'd failed her so miserably that night he hadn't even been able to convince her to put on a seat belt. "She was thrown from the car after it left the road, but she was still alive when the ambulance came. She was drunk so I told the police I was driving. I didn't want her to get a DUI."

"You were protecting her," Sara stated, getting it right and wrong at the same time. If he'd succeeded in protecting her, Chrissy never would have gotten behind the wheel. "But there's something I don't understand. Why do you think of yourself as a murderer?"

He leaned back in the chair, wondering if he had the courage to share the rest of the sordid story. She reached out, covering his hand with hers, and he started to talk.

"Things between Chrissy and me weren't good after we left Indigo Springs. I worked long hours and she was home alone a lot. She was always accusing me of sleeping around. It wasn't true, but that didn't seem to matter. It got to where I couldn't live like that anymore, especially because I didn't love her." He paused, then added, "That's the worst part, that I never loved her."

She squeezed his hand, silently encouraging him to continue.

"So I told her I wanted to break up. She got into my car and went tearing out of the driveway. I finally got a friend to drive me around looking for her. We found her in a bar." He fell silent, remembering how Chrissy had staggered out to the parking lot, crying and yelling.

"I still don't get it," Sara said. "Why blame yourself for what happened?"

"Because I didn't take the keys from her. I didn't want to make any more waves so I shut up and got in the car with her. I just wanted to get her home so she could sober up."

"What happened wasn't your fault!" Sara cried.

"Yeah," Michael said. "It was."

"No, Michael. It wasn't." Her eyes pleaded with him to believe her. "You can't hold yourself responsible for the decisions other people make. Chrissy made her own choices."

"I could have stopped her from driving."

"Maybe, but maybe not. If you'd driven home, she might have gotten back in the car and driven off again. And what's to say she wouldn't have gotten drunk again the next day?" She enunciated the next three words slowly and carefully. "You weren't responsible."

"She never would have left Indigo Springs if not for me," Michael said stubbornly, unable to let go of the guilt he'd held on to for so long. "Her father held me responsible for that."

"You don't know that she wouldn't have left," Sara argued. "You said she was headstrong. Besides, Mr. Coleman forgave you, the way you forgave your aunt. So why can't you forgive yourself?"

She gazed at him the way she always did, leaving no doubt that she believed in him. After a decade of self recrimination, it took only a small leap of faith for it to dawn on him it was time he started believing in himself.

He turned her hand over and traced her palm with the pad of his thumb, letting go of the guilt, gratitude nearly overwhelming him. "I don't deserve your support when I was such a jerk to you."

"I can't even agree with that," she said. "It took me a while, but I figured out you only said those things so I wouldn't have anything more to do with you. I know you were trying to protect me. I know you care about me."

That was an understatement, but he wasn't ready to put a name to what he felt. "I'm sorry, Sara. For everything."

She smiled at him then, more with her eyes than her lips. "I know."

He got off the porch swing, held out a hand and pulled her into his arms. She came willingly, touching his cheek, gazing at him with an expression that was both tender and sad. He had a crazy desire to tell her he'd refuse the Peace Corps assignment if she'd come with him to a place he could start a new life.

But he couldn't.

He wouldn't.

Her life was in Indigo Springs.

He lowered his head and poured everything he couldn't say into his kiss. He took note of the silkiness of her hair, the softness of her skin, the breathiness of her sigh. Storing memories to last a lifetime.

All they'd have was this single night, because he was still leaving in the morning.

SARA WALKED DOWN the hospital corridor late the next morning, blinking to keep her eyes dry. She hadn't given in to tears a few hours ago when Michael had left her bed, and she wouldn't now.

It struck her as ironic that her body could be sated from last night's lovemaking while her spirit felt bereft, but the feeling would pass. She'd lived without Michael before. She could live without him again.

She would content herself with the knowledge that she'd helped him slay his demons. Wherever he found himself living, whether it be Africa or the Middle East or South America, he'd be a happier man than when she'd met him.

Sara would be happy again, too.

She just wouldn't be happy today.

Today her mind was so full of Michael she couldn't retain the most rudimentary information, such as the room number the receptionist at the front desk had provided.

"Excuse me." She flagged down a young nurse who was about to bustle past her. "Could you tell me what room Quincy Coleman is in?"

Recognition filled the nurse's face. "The man who got rescued from the woods?"

"Yes."

"Room 217." She gestured to a room at the end of the hall. "I just left him though, so I know he's asleep."

"How is he?"

"Remarkably resilient. He was dehydrated when they brought him in, and it'll take a while for that broken bone to heal, but he's rebounding nicely." The nurse indicated the bouquet of daisies Sara clutched. "Are those for him?"

"Yes," Sara said. "Could you take them for me?"

"I'm on my rounds right now. You can leave them at the nurses' station. Or, better yet, give them to his wife. She's around the corner in our waiting area."

Sara had no intention of taking the nurse's suggestion. "Thanks."

She waited until the nurse disappeared into a nearby patient's room before turning back the way she'd come, in the opposite direction of the waiting room.

She hadn't gotten five steps when she heard

the tap of heels on linoleum. "Ms. Brenneman! Wait!"

Jill Coleman hurried after her, her hair out of place and her clothes rumpled, as though she'd spent the night in a chair. "I heard you talking to the nurse."

Sara thrust the flowers at Mrs. Coleman. She briefly debated explaining why she'd brought them, but her rationale was murky even to herself. If she had to put her reason into words, she'd say they were a thank-you for helping Michael put the past behind him. "I'd be grateful if you gave him these."

Mrs. Coleman took the daisies, but barely glanced at them, her upper teeth chewing her lower lip, something obviously on her mind.

"You probably figured out the women's club canceled your speech because of me," she said. "I'll fix it. I'll get you back on the schedule."

Sara nodded, figured there was nothing more for the two of them to talk about and started to turn.

"No, no. Don't go yet," Mrs. Coleman said, stopping Sara with the urgency in her voice. She was clutching the flowers so tightly Sara thought the stems might break. "I don't have any right to ask this of you, but I was hoping you could apologize to Michael Donahue for me."

The older woman's chest expanded before she finished in a rush. "I put that golf towel in his trunk after I used it to clean up the blood in the kitchen. I knew it was wrong, but I was so sure he was guilty."

Sara should have figured out on her own the puzzle of who planted the false evidence, but hadn't. The woman was obviously trying to make amends, but she'd picked the wrong person. "Why didn't you apologize to him yourself?"

"I couldn't face him. Not after what Quincy and I accused him of." She put a hand to her face. "And to think, he wasn't even driving the car."

"So your husband told you Chrissy was driving that night," Sara concluded.

"He told me everything, even about Chrissy calling and asking to come home." She sniffed, struggling to hold back tears. "He blames himself for telling her she could never come home, but she must have known he didn't mean it. The two of them, they were a lot alike."

Sara thought Mrs. Coleman had the same stubborn tendencies and couldn't stop herself from saying, "I hope you don't blame him for her death."

"I don't," she said. "We all make mistakes. We were wrong to hold Michael responsible for

Chrissy's accident. And I was wrong to put that towel in his car. I just hope he doesn't go to the police, but I wouldn't blame him if he did."

"Michael wouldn't do that," Sara said, "but I can't tell him anything for you. He's leaving town this morning."

Mrs. Coleman's eyes grew wide and her mouth fell open. "But I thought you two were a couple."

Sara cleared her throat, ignoring the pain that felt as though it was slicing her heart in two. "It didn't work out between us."

"There are plenty of reasons you shouldn't take my advice but indulge an old lady," she said. "Quincy and I spent the last eight years apart instead of helping each other get through the worst time of our lives. If I've learned anything this past week, it's that if you love somebody you work it out."

"But I don't…" Sara voice trailed off, the denial dying on her lips. The truth hit her like a thunderbolt.

The reason she felt this raw ache where her heart should be was because the man she loved—the man she very possibly had loved since she saw him rescue that boy on the river—was gone.

And she'd done absolutely nothing to stop him from going.

She backed down the hall, mumbling a hasty apology. "I'm sorry, but I've got to go."

She didn't stick around to find out if Mrs. Coleman was through talking. Neither did she get out her cell phone because what she had to tell Michael needed to be said face to face.

If she hurried, she might get to Felicia Feldman's house before he left town. If not, she'd track him down. Even if she had to go to Ghana to find him.

Because she loved Michael Donahue.

And love changed everything.

MICHAEL BREATHED IN the clean, river-scented air and let the babbling sound of the white water wash over him.

The beauty of the Lehigh River had always had the power to reach deep down inside him with a soothing hand, bringing him solace even when he was at his most troubled.

It was easy to understand why he'd sought the comfort the river offered when he was a teenager. Simpler still to figure out why the river had been his first stop when he returned to town.

Explaining why he was here now, when he should be on the road putting distance between himself and the town he'd hated for so long, was more complicated.

He shouldn't need to be soothed.

Quincy Coleman had stopped blaming him for Chrissy's death. Chief Jackson had started thinking of him as a good citizen instead of a likely suspect. And, although they'd never be friends, even Kenny Grieb had admitted he was wrong about him.

No, it wasn't because of any of those three men that he was here at the river. They weren't the people who would still be in his heart once he left Indigo Springs.

That list was growing.

Johnny Pollock and his dad. Aunt Felicia. Sara.

He tried to take a breath, but the realization that he loved Sara seemed to have knocked the wind out of him.

He'd known he loved her for a while, but admitting it meant acknowledging he didn't want to live without her. It meant asking her to leave Indigo Springs with him and preparing himself to hear her say no.

The crunching sound of footsteps in the woods cut into his thoughts. He turned and there was Sara, looking as lovely as when he'd first seen her at the wedding.

And nearly as well-dressed.

She'd dispensed with the stylish cropped jackets she was fond of wearing, but her tailored blouse and pencil-slim skirt were suitable for a courtroom. She even had her hair up in a slick, professional style.

He gaped at her, half believing he'd conjured her up out of sheer want.

"I'm so glad you haven't left yet." She sounded breathless, as though she'd been rushing. He glanced down at her feet. Heels. "I was on my way to your aunt's to try to catch you, but then I saw the PT Cruiser parked along the road and I knew you'd be here. I couldn't let you go until I told you something."

She was talking too fast, more like her receptionist Laurie than herself. He hadn't been aware of moving toward her, but he must have been because she was suddenly near enough to touch.

He covered her lips with three of his fingers, staunching her flow of words.

"I need to tell you something first." Now that he'd accepted the truth, the three words were like a wall of water that could no longer be held back by a dam. "I love you."

Her lips curved upward, her eyes lit up and she grabbed both of his hands. "That's what I was going to tell you. But that's not all. I'll come with you, Michael. Wherever you decide to go. I'll even apply to the Peace Corps if it means we can be together."

He'd been prepared to ask exactly that of her but the reality of what she'd be giving up struck him. "What about your law practice?"

"It's barely gotten off the ground," she said. "I can put it on hold and start over someplace else."

"Do you mean you're willing to give up Indigo Springs? For me?"

"Yes," she said without hesitation.

"But you love it here." He could barely believe he was arguing with her.

"I love you more," she said. "Indigo Springs is just a place."

Except that's not the way Michael had long thought of the town. It had been a symbol of the mistakes he'd made, an embodiment of the pain he'd lived with.

Just a place.

"No," he said forcefully. "You can't come with me."

Her mouth dropped open, the smile disappearing from her eyes to be replaced by what looked like pain.

"You can't come," he said, rushing to finish his thought, "because I'm staying."

"You are?"

"I love you too much to ask you to give up your job and your home. It makes more sense for me to stay than for you to leave," he said. "I can work for the Pollocks. Or start my own business. Or find a nonprofit where I can do just as much good at home as I can overseas."

He hadn't considered those possibilities before this minute, but they were all perfectly viable.

Sara laid a hand against his cheek, her eyes filled with concern. "Why would you offer to stay in a place that's brought you so much unhappiness?"

"Because you're right, Sara. It's just a place. People are what matter and this town has a fair number of people I care about." He stopped, realizing something even more important. "Even so, I'm not going to let anyone else decide what's best for me. I'm going to take a page from your book and listen to my heart."

She still didn't look convinced. "But can you ever be happy here?"

A great blue heron suddenly appeared in the clear sky, gracefully flapping its wings. Michael had no way of knowing whether it was the same heron he'd seen the day he rescued the boy, but he liked to think it was.

"I'm already happy here," Michael told Sara. "The town is a different, better place with you in it."

The worry lines on her face smoothed. She

looped her arms around his neck, the radiance back in her expression.

"If you're sure," she said, smiling.

"I'm very sure," Michael said. "From now on, my home is where you are."

And then, as the heron came to rest on the exposed surface of a nearby rock and the white water of the Lehigh splashed harmlessly around it, he kissed her.

* * * * *

Don't miss the next
RETURN TO INDIGO SPRINGS
Superromance from acclaimed author
Darlene Gardner—
coming in May 2009!

Harlequin is 60 years old,
and Harlequin Blaze is celebrating!
After all, a lot can happen in 60 years,
or 60 minutes…or 60 seconds!
Find out what's going down in Blaze's
heart-stopping new miniseries,
FROM 0 TO 60!
Getting from "Hello" to "How was it?"
can happen fast….

Here's a sneak peek of the first book,
A LONG, HARD RIDE
by Alison Kent.
Available March 2009.

"Is that for me?" Trey asked.

Cardin Worth cocked her head to the side and considered how much better the day already seemed. "Good morning to you, too."

When she didn't hold out the second cup of coffee for him to take, he came closer. She sipped from her heavy white mug, hiding her grin and her giddy rush of nerves behind it.

But when he stopped in front of her, she made the mistake of lowering her gaze from his face to the exposed strip of his chest. It was either give him his cup of coffee or bury her nose against him and breathe in. She remembered so clearly how he smelled. How he tasted.

She gave him his coffee.

After taking a quick gulp, he smiled and said, "Good morning, Cardin. I hope the floor wasn't too hard for you."

The hardness of the floor hadn't been the

problem. She shook her head. "Are you kidding? I slept like a baby, swaddled in my sleeping bag."

"In my sleeping bag, you mean."

If he wanted to get technical, yeah. "Thanks for the loaner. It made sleeping on the floor almost bearable." As had the warmth of his spooned body, she thought, then quickly changed the subject. "I saw you have a loaf of bread and some eggs. Would you like me to cook breakfast?"

He lowered his coffee mug slowly, his gaze as warm as the sun on her shoulders, as the ceramic heating her hands. "I didn't bring you out here to wait on me."

"You didn't bring me out here at all. I volunteered to come."

"To help me get ready for the race. Not to serve me."

"It's just breakfast, Trey. And coffee." Even if last night it had been more. Even if the way he was looking at her made her want to climb back into that sleeping bag. "I work much better when my stomach's not growling. I thought it might be the same for you."

"It is, but I'll cook. You made the coffee."

"That's because I can't work at all without caffeine."

"If I'd known that, I would've put on a pot as soon I got up."

"What time *did* you get up?" Judging by the sun's position, she swore it couldn't be any later than seven now. And, yeah, they'd agreed to start working at six.

"Maybe four?" he guessed, giving her a lazy smile.

"But it was almost two…" She let the sentence dangle, finishing the thought privately. She was quite sure he knew exactly what time they'd finally fallen asleep after he'd made love to her.

The question facing her now was where did this relationship—if you could even call it *that*—go from here?

* * * * *

Cardin and Trey are about to find out that
great sex is only the beginning….
Don't miss the fireworks!
Get ready for
A LONG, HARD RIDE
by Alison Kent.
Available March 2009,
wherever Blaze books are sold.

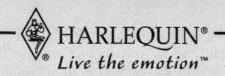

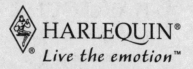

HARLEQUIN®
INTRIGUE®

BREATHTAKING ROMANTIC SUSPENSE

Shared dangers and passions lead to electrifying
romance and heart-stopping suspense!

Every month, you'll meet six new heroes
who are guaranteed to make your spine tingle
and your pulse pound. With them you'll enter
into the exciting world of Harlequin Intrigue—
where your life is on the line
and so is your heart!

THAT'S INTRIGUE—
ROMANTIC SUSPENSE
AT ITS BEST!

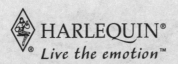

HARLEQUIN®
® *Live the emotion*™

Harlequin® Historical
Historical Romantic Adventure!

*Imagine a time of chivalrous
knights and unconventional ladies,
roguish rakes and impetuous
heiresses, rugged cowboys
and spirited frontierswomen—
these rich and vivid tales will
capture your imagination!*

*Harlequin Historical . . .
they're too good to miss!*